SCALE

A BARNACLE BOOK
RARE BIRD BOOKS
LOS ANGELES, CALIF.

SC▲LE

A NOVEL

Keith Buckley

THIS IS A GENUINE BARNACLE BOOK
THE ORIGINAL IMPRINT OF RARE BIRD BOOKS

453 South Spring Street, Suite 302
Los Angeles, Calif. 90013
rarebirdbooks.com

Distributed by Publishers Group West,
a division of the Perseus Books Group
Printed in the United States of America

10 9 8 7 6 5 4 3 2

Publisher's Cataloging-in-Publication data

Names: Buckley, Keith, author.
Title: Scale: a novel / by Keith Buckley.
Description: First trade paperback original edition. | A Barnacle Book. |
New York ; Los Angeles : Rare Bird Books, 2015.
Identifiers: ISBN 978-1-940207-99-5
Subjects: Musicians—Fiction. | Bands (Music)—Fiction. | Rock music—Fiction.
| Family—Fiction. | BISAC : FICTION / Literary. |
Classification: LCC PS3602.U2624 S33 2015 | DDC 813.6—dc23

Book Design by Robert Schlofferman

CHAPTER ONE

COINCIDENTALLY, I HAPPENED UPON A bead of light. After prematurely returning home from Australia where nothing moved me—where I found no inexplicable splendor on mountain or sand; where words cowered in dry corners rather than being rendered insufficient by rampant awe—there was a droplet of illumination left for me in a brochure outside of our building, blown up against the fence that followed the sidewalk to the door. Though neither my name nor address were on it, it was written in a language that spoke to a very specific and personal looming darkness. That darkness—the one this surreptitious letter acknowledged—had recently discovered me again holed up in my hotel room where I was too weak and too broken in too many places to refuse it entry. To find this piece of paper just days later was a welcomed rope dropped by unfamiliar hands from the top of my empty well, and though typically a staunch empirical skeptic, I could not help but wonder as I scanned the pamphlet that cold morning—*What if...?*

It was a simple enough question, but one I had never dared to ask myself, most likely due to the paralyzing uncertainty it promised to bring with it. Yet, standing in my front yard, an antennae snapped in half along with my rib, my jaw still stinging, my tooth cracked, and the ring around my left eye gradually shifting colors from deep purples and reds to light yellows and greens like the feathers of some exotic bird deep into a mating dance, I knew that a drastic and thorough overhaul was absolutely necessary if I hoped to continue forward. The field could not be razed as long as I was still dumbly tending to the infected crops. Asking myself *What if...?* as I skimmed the testimonials meant first admitting to myself that I was wrong about myself, which was a feeling not unlike coming to consciousness after talking in your sleep to someone who lays next to you and shares not the same dream. Your self-assuredness in issues pertinent to the entire underworld that you bring to the surface with proud Herculean strength eventually dwindles down to a drowsy relationship with a personal sphere of cloudy hints, and as logic arrives and attempts to quiet your enthusiastic candor, the *knowingness* eventually vanishes completely, your awakening leaving you to feel lonely, distant, confused, and ashamed as the very real place you just traveled from retreats into mist like an indifferent city bus keeping to its own schedule while you run desperately after it until you can run no more and stand defeated in the street.

To make matters more difficult, how does one convince themself that they are not the things that define them? It's like using language in order to express the idea that language does not exist or painting a picture of nothingness given only the colors that something-ness has afforded you. We are not wont to accept such an absurdity in the presence of overwhelming evidence to the contrary or to suffer an affront to our identity from a voice infinitely tinier than our elephantine selves, but then again, I repeated to myself, *What if...?*

After three decades of life with the support of two happily married parents, the unconditional, though never vocally confessed love of a younger sister, and few friends that remained virtually unchanged since high school—not to mention a system of beliefs heard, understood, entertained, and adopted throughout my formative years which were now reinforced daily both on stage and in interviews in my adulthood—I was not eager to admit that the results I had recently come upon might not support the theory I originally posited. I was too deep undercover to casually reemerge as the man I was before I went down in; had worked far too hard to lock up the lab because of a hypothetical. However, I felt—or rather some small part of me signaled at feeling—that there was a molecular lie being told that had fooled even the greatest chemist.

I clutched the paper and mindfully went inside having made a decision that felt like the first decision I had ever made. It was one that began as a ripple in a stagnant pond of old energy and registered in something greater than my brain, moving through scaffoldings sturdier than my bones. There was a child in me who needed to walk for no other reason than it was his instinct to finally live upright.

CHAPTER TWO

THE MOTHER—OR THE QUEEN OR WHATEVER name you choose to call her—has many children. All she has ever done is bear children and her desire reaches no further than guiding one to replace its elder in a transcendent state of pure bliss. The mother (or the queen) has sat pinnacled above a whispering black stream since before there was time. As has always been and always will be, when an unwitting piece of misfit glory drifts obliviously below, she ceases to be, she plucks it from the current in her divine hands and shapes it carefully and purposefully under her maternal third eye to resemble something of herself. Then, the mother allows the child one last drink from the water that has carried it so that it in turn may now be the vessel that possesses the spring, and she places it gently down atop the same endless peak she inhabits. When she returns her attention to being, all of her children bask in the radiance that emanates from her. Being and creating are all she can do. The truly wise know nothing but selflessness.

But one day her children will become aware there are other children, and at that moment they can be a child of the mother's no longer. They will, if they are true to their new reason, separate from her and venture bravely down from the crest and outward through the eons to seek what it means to be young no more, carrying with them a new vision of fate and a vague memory of the essence of that first eternal stream. You, however, are a dawdling relic idling grotesquely in the fertile soil of forever readying seeds. You are without vision and oblivious to the new will of the fellow child. You are without language and, therefore, without song. You sleep often but dream irreverently and provide evidence in favor of the claim made by those in motion that we are not all descended from great things. Your very presence is an affront to her mastery, for when she is undone with joy and unified with absolute rapture, your meaninglessness casts an indolent beam of shade. You bring rumors and you challenge her efficiency, and so you must leave. You are owed nothing. Go earn love.

CHAPTER THREE

THE HYPNOTHERAPISTS OFFICE WAS UNDER a dental practice in a plaza by the college about twenty minutes north of my house. When I arrived, I parked outside of the building and tried to collect any remaining familiar pieces of myself in order to better understand which ones no longer fit and must be either altered or eradicated completely. Like a temperamental schoolboy who was faced with an impending curfew, my identity was in a snarling fit of rage. It was aware that its time was limited and it longed violently to stay in the presence of the things that strengthened it. It brought forth shame by reminding me of how foolish hypnotism seemed, how weak I was giving my time and money to someone I once would have deemed a charlatan, and how stupid I would look to my fans if they found me here or knew of what I was doing. It threatened me with a loss of creativity once all cynicism was vanquished, and promised loneliness at the onset of a venture down roads without companions that did something far more hopeless than dead end: they went on forever. It mocked my complete lack of a real understanding of who I had ever been and my outlandishly unreal hopes of ever changing, and it spit and hissed at the inchoate need for tranquility that I placed in its cage. It would not go humbly into the past, that was for certain. But what too was certain—and what was made even clearer by the elaborate protest that I watched flare up—was that all I had to do, all anything inside of me or out was asking that I do in a language of coincidences and vague signaling, was to close the curtain, shut out my own internal voice, and tend—finally—to the condition of my patient but estranged heart.

I walked through the front of the complex and found a directory which informed me that the hypnosis clinic was set apart from the other offices in a basement hallway, which didn't necessarily comfort me but seemed appropriate given its questionable status as an effective psychological procedure in my old eyes. From what little I knew about people who claimed to be hypnotists, I, too, would have opted to put them in a damp basement. As I descended the steps I distinctly heard a woman's voice and followed it into an office in which three televisions were playing three different testimonial videos. The receptionist looked up at me as I entered in disbelief that someone had entered, I told her that I was there to get an assessment like the one I had read about in the ad.

"To quit smoking?"

"No, I'm still gonna do that. I need help..." And in a pause that felt like years, I realized that I had no specific idea of what I was there to receive. I had not actually sounded it out with words that would convey a message to another human being. I began to dream up multiple ways in which I could be saved. I was in the bathroom of a bar at 2:30 in the morning buying drugs with rent money and trying to explain to her that if the house of alcohol was destroyed all the sins it sheltered would be destroyed as well. I was alone in a hotel room off the map masturbating to an old flame's Facebook profile and asking for help controlling a maniacal longing for physical contact. I was onstage, at a loss for words, the whole world spinning and unclear and I pleaded with her to help me find the confidence required to stop dismantling myself for the sake of applause. I was towering over Frank this time, whisking his brain and skull into a thick broth with a rusty iron rod in front of a throng of cheering onlookers and begging her to convince me that his blood will not bring back the things he stole. But in one last surge of sheer force, honor unleashed a thunderous howl and I cowered. I would be no one without the things that helped me forget me.

"...Dealing with stress," I lied. And so began my new trip on the wrong foot with an outdated map.

CHAPTER FOUR

I F I HADN'T FAILED TO NOTICE THAT THE APPLICATION I sent to Syracuse University referred to Virginia Tech in the final paragraph—or if I had written an altogether separate essay rather than just lazily interchanging names despite the two presenting the same exact question on the application form— it would make sense to assume that events in my life would be drastically altered, possibly steered down a path of much less internal resistance, one walked with a more natural stride rather than this one that began by jumping nervously between only apparently reliable patches of ground shaped by circumstances of harsh mental weather, emotional eruptions, and corrosion of reason. In another universe maybe that alteration was realized, and instead of stumbling cross-eyed through throwaway classes and developing an addiction to both cigarettes and the warmth of nervous adrenaline that partnered with new girls, I was aimed true north with healthy lungs and the steady, high love of the girl I'd known since I was a kid. In dreams maybe that version of myself comes to me and here, with the things I've used to build the world that pertains to me, he is allowed to exist and play for some time while I do nothing more than pay slight attention to the rustling stream that only gets quieter with each step I take toward the horizon until it inevitably vanishes.

There was no particular reason for me to leave Ithaca, New York other than to hush the goading voices that instruct all teenagers to forsake their home at the first sign that the bread is growing stale, but I refused to believe I was not unique and confessed to Aaron that living there "was like sleeping in a bed with a woman that loved me no longer" as if the quaint municipality offended me personally and Aaron, as he typically did when I told him about the disingenuous things I had written, rolled his eyes. I had little experience with women and I lived with my parents in a suburb and drove a car that my father made the payments on. I could have gone anywhere really, given that the only direction I cared about moving was out, but I chose Virginia Tech based on nothing more than the picture of the campus on the front of the catalogue that sat on a desk in the office of my guidance councilor neither aimed at nor addressed to any one student specifically.

So, in August of 1997, I stood in front of the East Ambler-Johnson building on the cusp of one of the most important transformative phase changes a person could ever go through, and I couldn't have been less aware. If I had really stopped to understand the scope of the moment rather than panting like an excited dog at the door to the wide-open backyard, I might have realized how difficult this all was for my mother and showed a little gratitude for her years of stern kindness by at least pretending to be sad. I didn't. I remained stoically self-absorbed and kept my eye on the glowing brass ring as my parents hugged me goodbye.

VT—located in Blacksburg, Virginia on the shore of a sea of timid hills that are eternally reddish orange in my memory—was an institution hidden in a womb-like valley where the single-celled nascent artist that I designed could germinate into the fully formed novelist I thought I longed to be. The campus would be my intellectual training facility where I would bolster the identity of "Poet" that I had finally chosen out of the thousand possibilities that gnashed their baby teeth at each other inside of me, lurching for the worm that I brought inward. They extended their thin necks trying to outreach each other upward and receive the sacred nutrients that would take them to the next day where they would again fight—this time amongst dead brethren—to make it to the next, the cycle repeating, their numbers dwindling, but their capabilities strengthening. When one remained, an able and concise image of myself would stand directly before me at the hill crest and I would remove my milky, untried skin and toil until we constellated, the old I and the eventual I, rendering ourselves eternally static. From that point on, there would be a template to which I could refer whenever doubt arose, a handbook scrawled by my genetics like commandments into the walls of the valleys of my thinking mind, an unflinching panacea immune to scrutiny that would serve me well in any intellectual or moral moment of doubt. And when the rock rolled away and I, as both the sculpture and sculptor emerged, a true artist would be loosed upon the world. Behold.

Before I turned away for good my father unlocked the trunk of the van and handed me a guitar case.

"Your hands are big enough now," he said, his voice shaking, unpracticed. I thanked him with a silent nod. Then I shook his hand, separated myself from mother, kissed Lilly's cheek as she sat wide-eyed in her wheelchair, and I went down in, vulnerable and unknown.

CHAPTER FIVE

OVER THE NEXT TWO MONTHS, MY ninety-minute sessions with a doctor named Singer revealed two remarkable new things. Firstly, a subtle doubt was discovered that, once noticed, began quietly knocking against the wrought iron gates of my own heavily fortified certainties threatening upheaval. Secondly, I was so lost that I was willing to entertain a shocking amount of palpable bullshit. There were three sessions where the doctor had simply given me headphones and left the room while the disembodied voice of an entirely different doctor attempted to alter my thought patterns with softly spoken suggestions only to return and charge me ten dollars for the CD I had just heard. On principle alone, the old me would have been outraged, demanding a refund, and storming out of the office in a fury of curse words and violence, but on the first occurrence of this injustice (the fourth session in), I was unable to immediately detect anything inside of me that demanded retribution. In fact, when that reliable dire wolf of pride was touched by an unfamiliar hand, it stood up only begrudgingly and showed its fangs—not as if to use them, but to feebly reassure me that they were in fact still there. Though its presence was obvious enough to give me cause to take a few steps back, this time there was something in its eyes that was less convincing. It growled lowly at the doctor—and at his terribly impersonal methods and at his obvious disinterest in the betterment of a paying patient—but only briefly, before retiring to the shadow in which it had always lived. And as it turned from us, I too turned away from it, for the first time unafraid to show it my defenseless back.

This moment was an extraordinary moment, for it was one in which I could feel from outside of what I thought of as myself. And I was not just placating my own violent temper with deceitful excuses or duplicitous promises of a far-off cure. I was fully aware in the present moment that I was being robbed of something valuable to me—my sense of self—and I genuinely didn't know if that was such a bad thing.

What timidly ventured out through me in the time between meetings with Dr. Singer was noticeable in the way that a quiet guest is as he stands in the back of the room at a party. It was obvious I was only at this point eavesdropping on the un-tormented, and while an observant few may have eyed me askance, most were so wrapped up their own joy that I could have been ten feet tall and still gone unseen. I was, however, trembling with an inner excitement as I calculated what felt like quantum leaps into experiences with which I had familiarity but no real knowledge. And if I could not stick my landing, the dejection I felt only registered as meaning there were now fewer possible wrongs, as if all opposing forces were drawn from sizable but finite reserve while those coordinating to aid intellectual and emotional evolution were innumerable.

I began retesting the roaring waters of life, compelled by a new resolute hope that one day I would no longer drown in them, but use them to carry me to wondrous depths. I was spending less and less time inside of my head and more time in my body, which at that point was, I discovered, grossly neglected and misshapen from over a decade of abuse at the hands of overgenerous drunk fans.

The baseless predictions of tragic and unwanted future outcomes, the fanatical planning of all possible reactions to all possible actions in order to assure an alignment with the immovable mental image of myself and the incessant laboring over past errors that occupied so much real estate inside my head that the present had nowhere to show itself, began to dissipate. What was once a thick, suffocating smoke was now a dirty cloud. The stone carapace that I had bedecked myself in began to crack and a dim glow was seen. The channels coursing through my brain that had been dug out by my heritage, by my social surroundings, by my education, by my desires, and by my idols, were dried up and becoming overgrown with new grasses while new, wandering paths were being formed by the persistent force of suggestion that stroked my subconscious. A new road appeared where formerly there was none.

It may not have been true. I may not have actually been a person worthy of love or acceptance by my friends and family and fans based on all the terrible things I had done, but what mattered was that I began to feel that by altering the world inside of me I could very slightly begin to tweak the calibrations of the real world that existed outside of me and cause it to respond to my will. From a source-less voice on a recording made by a man I'd never met whom had no knowledge of my existence (and who may have himself no longer even existed), I was given another cool, refreshing, drop of pure light.

CHAPTER SIX

MY FIRST AND CONCURRENTLY LAST few weeks at VT were rife with productivity, though an intestinal tract works harder than most organs and still only manages to create mostly shit, so whether there was any merit to my work was arguable. The book of short stories I had written and titled *Divining Machines* still sits in a box in a closet of my parents' house, and the songs I wrote and planned to put on a demo never actually made it further than a few parties when I was handed an acoustic guitar. They did, however, lead to some spirited sexual encounters with a sophomore named Jennifer, which was as good as any standing ovation.

That first pathetic orgasm taught me above all else that *acting like* and *being* were indistinguishable states, perhaps separated only at a quantum level by the intelligence of the observer present. The truth is subjective, something internalized and interpreted and is really only as sturdy as our argument for it. The world had just recently watched as a murderer walked away a free man based on this tenet, so to the impressionable population around me—them, those mindlessly sketched extras in my narrative who had only a few unclear visions of a laughable version of paradise—I would appear not as the sum of parts measured out by indifferent generations before me, but as the materialized intent of my own mind perpetually building its own destiny. Already, I could hear unnecessary chunks of marble fall away from what would someday be seen as me and I was overjoyed.

There was nothing that could turn my concentration away from the plans I had drawn up and laid out before me, and if there was, it would only be to reinforce the perception of the eventual masterpiece at its unveiling. I cut myself off from most people and hungrily took in the work of the beat writers like bad cigarette smoke and, once I found a grocery store off campus that was fooled by my fake ID, took in bad cigarette smoke with even worse whiskey. I wrote poems. I played my guitar. I dreamt. And though I efficiently ran through the exercises of collegiate life, the curriculum was just a muddy stream that I waded through in order to reach a more distant shore. By night I edited feverishly, aping the gorgeous prose of my new idols until I managed to get a poem published in a local magazine that I submitted to after reading an ad for it on the wall in the Center for Student Life and another in the college paper itself. These small but important achievements nurtured a hungry and dangerous life force that lurked somewhere underneath, representing a potential that could be moved into being if given what it desired. It was, as I now felt certain, beginning its ascent up the opposite side of same unseeable astral hill that I too marched up.

It was to my utmost dismay, then, when my progress was not just halted but altogether undone by a political science teacher named Tiller who accused me of cheating on an exam only two weeks into my first semester. The accusation was based on an exceptional grade in the face of what should have been a mutually exclusive poor attendance record, though he and the head of the department felt them to be directly correlated and no argument could persuade them otherwise. On top of all of this, in order for me to insure the nearly perfect grade on his paper, Professor Tiller concocted a story packed with the kind of cunning and foresight reserved for Victorian-era jewel thieves and one I only fully understood from the elevated angle of hindsight after it was explained to me. One which was light-years away from the truth of the eerie, unfortunate, and completely arbitrary jumble of unlikely events that conspired against me in a perfect storm.

I returned from a weekend spent at a new friend's house in September to find a voicemail from Professor Tiller himself saying that he needed to speak with me immediately. He didn't say exactly why, but I assumed that he probably wanted me to tutor other students based solely on the fact that I experienced exactly zero moments of doubt while taking his exam about two weeks prior. Though I found his drawl too slow to be sufferable and rarely attended his uninspired lectures, I had studied diligently for his exam in a coffee-fueled solitary overnight session and went into the classroom that next morning as confident in my mastery of the information as I was when I walked out of it two hours later, seeing as how he had basically used the same questions that were in the Study Guide at the end of each chapter. The conversation that began when he handed me my scan-tron sheet with a comically large letter "F" circled in thick red marker as I took a seat in front of his office desk, however, was a little different than what I expected.

"What is this?" I asked, visibly stunned.

"That's your exam."

"It can't be. I knew the answer to every question."

"Well, mostly all of the answers are right," he said smugly, trailing off as his cigarette-stained mustache indicated his thin, dry lips were smirking underneath it. "But they're not *your* answers. They're your friend Laura's, the girl you sat next to. I know because I have the sign-in sheet," he said knowingly, assuming that I might begin feeling trapped. However, since I hadn't any insight into what he was getting at, I felt nothing but utter confusion.

The story as he told it was set into motion for him when he returned to his office after administering the exam and began grading. About ten minutes later (the time it took me to walk back to my room) he received a call from me (which he had), telling him that I had forgotten to indicate which version of the exam I had been given (which I did) but that it was definitely version D (which it was) and I was sorry for being so absent-minded. This, apparently, raised a red flag for him because, as he went back to make note of it, he noticed that I had been seated next to a student named Laura (which I was). In fact, it was a happy coincidence that the only friend I had made in that class had one of the only open seats available near the back corner of the room which was set up that morning with ten or so rows across, an even number of desks in each row. Unbeknownst to me or anyone else in the class, Professor Tiller thought he could more effectively prevent cheating if he made more versions of the exam than there were desks in a row. That way, the first seat of the first row would get version A, the first seat of the second row would get B, and so on. So when he realized that Laura had marked her exam as version D right there in the room that morning, there was no possible way I could have had it as well.

So he thought.

What he revealed to me as I sat there genuinely bewildered by the facts presented thus far, was a description of the events leading up to that moment as he saw them.

In his simple mind, he had formulated a thesis of historical significance that rivaled the solution of Fermat's Enigma, one that appeared in a brief flash of genius after long nights poring over dusty books in his lab in a castle atop a hill. Essentially, what he had determined was that I sat next to Laura based on a plan she and I had formulated prior to the exam, which went as follows: She was to enter the classroom first and reserve me a seat next to her, an action so unthinkably brazen it just might work. Next, I would politely take the exam I was handed from the poor, unwitting pawn in front of me and inconspicuously put it aside entirely— *intentionally failing to indicate which form I was given.* Then, using the razor-sharp vision that my glasses endowed me with (and at this point he actually said, "I don't remember ever seeing you wear glasses before"), I would copy Laura's answers onto my scantron form, changing a few here and there so as not to appear too obvious. After they were handed in, we would rendezvous outside of the classroom where she would tell me what version she had. I would then return to my dorm, make a phone call explaining my carelessness, and all would end well.

"However!" he declared excitedly, "what ruined your plan was the unknown fact that I had made more versions than there were seats in a row. You and Laura would not have had the same versions."

He sat back on the corner of his desk and placed his hands upon his bent knee, half expecting me to confess or at least be impressed by his calculated methods. But the truth is that we were given the same exams. That's all there is to it. And to further confuse this uncanny scenario, I really did make the innocent mistake of simply not noticing that there was a place at the top of the form where I was suppose to indicate which version I had, the reason being that I had absolutely no expectation for there being different forms at all. Why would I? It wasn't tradition, or edict. Admittedly, it was an *unknown fact* that numerous versions were made but it was also as unknown that he made any more than one, so why would I be compelled to intentionally leave it blank only to pretend I had a copy I didn't afterward? And if I did somehow know in advance that there would be different exams but *foolishly* thought that they were going to be even in number, why didn't

I copy off whomever I happened to be sitting next to, given that my glasses were only worn to see someone else's answers from a distance? Why would I include anyone else at all in my master plan to see better?

All that really happened was that I randomly chose the wrong seat in a row where a notoriously dense professor most likely accidentally stacked two of the same versions on top of each other before handing a stack of them to the first seat, failed to notice that my exam had a letter of the top, aced the exam I studied hard for, and unexpectedly ran into Laura on my walk back to my room where we discussed the test and whether or not I had the one with the *impossible first question.*

"I don't know," I answered. "Were there different ones?"

"Yeah. I saw they were different as I passed them back to the guy behind me."

"Shit. I didn't notice. He's not going to know which key to use to grade mine." I said as I picked up the pace a little, contemplating whether or not I could make it to a phone before I could return to his office if I decided to turn around. "What was the first question?"

"Something about the Jacksonian View of Democracy which I had never even fucking heard of."

"Yeah, that was my first question, too. So what version was that?"

"I had version D."

And that was it. I returned to my room and did what I thought would make his job easier by calling him immediately. I never thought about it again until that day. I still don't know exactly how Laura and I got the same test, but if I had to guess I would have said that it was the rampant hatred God had for me once again boiling over and cascading onto my stupidly peaceful routine, his hard foot on the top of my head drowning me entirely in the very elements I had once idiotically used for support.

I said nothing. I was a dead vehicle, one that could make no sound or movement until given something substantial to run on and aimed somewhere—*anywhere*—by a more knowledgeable operator. I was completely devoid of any purpose for a few moments, an overheated vessel stranded in a desert that stretched infinitely in all directions, a bizarre intersection that promised nothing but more nothing. Then I started laughing, honestly considering it to be some rude joke perpetuated by the entire state of Virginia when my brain failed to register it as a possible event in a universe operating under certain laws that wouldn't allow for such a disfiguration.

"I'm moving to have you expelled," he said.

Then I went numb. Instantly, and with more clarity than I had ever realized anything before despite the vacuous pit I was suddenly gazing into, I understood that I was just another one of life's insipid moveable pieces, remotely controlled and barely minded. It was a cold, ghastly Eureka Moment that exploded with a groan and spread throughout my severely limited realm of understanding like a wave of polluted oil, heavy and breathtaking. A suffocating futility fell upon me as my brain tried desperately to contact spirit for permission to shift away from what the violent march of time dropped at its feet like the limp body of a dead man, groping desperately at ecstasy, but spirit denied, and body and mind found themselves tethered to the wretched earth and silenced by a meaninglessness that had eluded my cognition. Under the cover of darkness, a cruel fate snuck quietly in through an unchecked possibility where there were no defenses—an outcome that I failed to guard by not recognizing it as a prospective version of the future—and God slit my throat as I slept. In my last moments, when chaos and all its unknown buried me, I saw the hole I left unfortified and cursed my own carelessness and stupidity, just as my lungs collapsed. What really were my certainties worth if they covered not every square inch of life's terrible land?

I returned to my room and laid on my bed in a deep disconnect. Professor Tiller had called after me something about a court date, but all senses worked to hush the outside world and forced me to have me to myself. It was there, at the base of the reflection cast inward by self-pity, that I noticed something I had never seen before: a translucent film had begun to form between where the world was and where it was meant to be, four gelatinous walls appearing around my awareness in the middle of a field, a hazy prison emerging and establishing parameters that only more absolutely marked the disparity between *mine* and *theirs*. In the layers of blue embryonic mucus I could see faded flashes of runny lightning and swirls of cool spit. New eyelids, ones now closed only when truly awake, would stand at the door to my deepest brain and show me all that was death.

I could feel my blood starting to freeze as Professor Tiller was called forth to stand before me, not on a plane in the world he had for so long comfortably navigated, but in a new one that erupted into existence like a photon that was located somehow past my eyes at the foot of the membrane that now shelled my spirit. He stood proud and defiant, but as I moved in closer I could faintly smell the sweat beginning to seep through his tender skin. I put both my hands on the front of his neck, and in them I could feel his terror swell as he became aware that his life—everyone he loved and everything he knew as true—now only existed as a temporary reflection in my distant, black, uncompromising eyes. Instinctually my fingers elongated, coiling themselves around its full circumference. Smooth and wet. Heaving forward and around. They interlocked and constricted. Then, the unmistakably high, sharp stench of piss.

"I am not as you see me," I hissed.

His eyes, those same accusatory bloodshot green eyes that broke into my soul and butted against everything I had built were forced opened wide and bulged from their sockets, scanning the room as if to find air in a place they hadn't thought to look. They found none. His throat emitted a sound like the squeezing of an empty plastic water bottle as he clawed at my stone arms. A trickle of blood timidly peeked from his nose—then became a stream, then became a river—rushing forward with a devastating excitability. I lapped at it with my thin, leathery tongue like I hadn't drank in weeks, every mouthful strengthening the unified muscle I was. It was refreshingly hot and tasted of rust.

"I am not as you think…"

His face was now the color of dusk and his lips swelled like two broken ankles. I eagerly sank my teeth into the bottom one and pulled it off. It didn't make a sound. Flaps of carelessly perforated skin dangled briefly from my mouth as I chewed it, but they too were consumed. I took the other lip in the same fashion exposing his flat yellow teeth. He stuck his tongue out and frantically waved it back and forth fruitlessly searching for the absent pieces of his face and as he did so I bit into that too, sucking it out of his mouth into mine. Once convinced I had the full extent of it between my teeth, I severed it from him. He had no air with which to carry a scream nor a tongue to crown it so he kicked and shook violently instead.

I saw my mother and my father's face with my mind's eye. The inconceivable disappointment they carried in their fine lines. Their son now a hive on the lawn, cracked in half by a nasty child with a stick standing triumphantly above. An entire kingdom vanquished in an afterthought. A bird with one wing sat doomed in its tree.

"I am only as I say."

A magisterial cry echoed. I recoiled my fingers from around his neck and as he stumbled back I fell upon him and straddled his chest, my thumbs pressing firmly into his eyes until they exploded at the back of their sockets. There is no crime without a witness. Tiller would go and take his idea of me as a liar and cheat with him and anyone that sympathized or saw me not as I said I was would have their eyes gouged out as well. There was no room in this world for opposite realities to coexist. Reality is not subject to interpretation. It just is, and everything else is not.

He emitted an inhuman sound. I smelled his shit as it filled his pants. I laughed and bit off his nose, tossing my head back and letting it slip down my throat, chomping mightily. The blood was everywhere. I rubbed my cheeks against his, my forehead and chin and nose gliding across the gaps in his face, cackling madly all the while. The soul that left his body saw me clamped onto its former neck, now open wide, drunkenly consuming the fluid that spewed forth in a rhythm dictated by its useless pulse. Then, with an erection as hard as diamond, I cracked through his chest and chewed up his heart. I had never before in my life seen death, but there, in my head, in that room that day it appeared as real as my own face and I came to fear it on a level deeper than hell itself. My meeting with Tiller was the last time I would ever be so unprepared for dark to fall. In abject blackness an artist was born anew.

CHAPTER SEVEN

BEGINNING IN AUGUST I HAD ABOUT TWENTY shows lined up at a few House of Blues and other decently sized venues that would stretch as far as Los Angeles and back. I was supposed to have two shorter runs in secondary markets in the time in between the end of my scheduled Australian run and then, but with all the problems I had in the studio I knew I was in no shape to hit the road and therefore lost out on a significant paycheck and valuable opportunities to promote the new record.

Though I was slowly recovering, there was still a part of me that went intentionally unexplored, the part where I had buried the humiliatingly vivid image of me laying bloodied and unconscious in a dimly lit Australian venue. Videos taken by onlookers were all over the Internet, so my embarrassment reached far beyond the borders of heavily guarded dignity and deep into the dark forest of public perception. If I chose to unearth it and stare at it for too long I knew that I might be moved backward through the loathsome caverns of wounded ego, relying solely on an irrational and all-powerful anger to guide me, so I felt it best to just let it be and distract myself in any way I could while I waited to be whole again. I could not let that awful weight cripple me any further, and as Dr. Singer said, there was no reason to remind myself of the past by holding vigil over those unnatural events, nor should I any longer devour myself from the inside out over the incredible weakness I had shown in being so easily bested or obsess over the fact that such unthinkable treachery had occurred in the proverbial public square after which the guilty walked, never to be tried. It did me no good in those weeks that followed to slink around and believe I was owed an apology, and even though it might have been the only thing strong enough to pull me from the canyon I was so eagerly racing toward the bottom of, it was not permitted by whatever horrible voices drove the man who pushed me there. I was out of his sight, and if I were to believe the things he barked at me as I passed in and out of consciousness on the floor of the venue lobby, I was certainly insignificant enough to be out of his mind. Whereas a few weeks prior I would have greeted death warmly and asked its help in finally ending my lonely descent, now I wondered if maybe I couldn't recruit life to try to do exactly the same thing.

If there was a karma, perhaps it would avenge me, and Frank's actions would echo forever and the beauty around him would hear its awful call and wince and turn away from him while I was given strength to move out of earshot and back to the higher ground I inhabited until the day we met. Of course if karma didn't, it would just reinforce my belief that karma wasn't, and though I would lose in the same way I had always lost, at least I would still be able to say that I knew it all along. Being able to accurately predict a constant loss is more rewarding than being unable to predict a sudden win. Being surprised is being made to look stupid and there was no state of being more despicable than the one occupied while looking stupid.

In the time I had at home to myself I found I was not as desperately seeking the company of friends as I typically would have been in the dwindling hours before I was called on by the greedy road. I was noticeably less frantic about consuming

Eddie's gossips and gripes and in this slowed jog I unearthed a surprisingly pleasant solitude—surprising because for as long as I could remember, fear of exclusion was the prevailing tendency that drove nearly everything I did. When I was young I more than once opted to piss in my own pants rather than go to the bathroom and miss a minute of the parties that my parents threw almost every summer weekend growing up. I refused sleep because it meant accepting the possibility that there was no more fun to be had, and as an adult that stubbornness translated into an appreciation for cocaine and other forms of speed. It was a stifling fear that without eyes upon me, without multiple witnesses to my existence, I had no alibi that proved I was alive. I would hoard experience in the basement of time like a deceased lover's belongings, convincing myself that one day, in order to save my life, I may need to dig up the "Eddie Breaks Beer Bottle Over the Head of Some Guy At Father Baker's" file. I hadn't seen my small circle of old friends in a while, and soon I would be leaving again. So where was my unhappy hunger for their lives? How was I able to sit comfortably alone on a Friday night gently strumming my guitar rather than going to the bar and struggling to devour the city all in one bite? Why was there a significant but indefinable distaste for their impassioned sermons about the glory of our shared teenage years? It hurt my heart to look upon them and feel no lust. My soul whispered rumors of estrangement.

It wasn't that I felt urged to move beyond them, for I still loved them dearly and in many senses they were masters from which I was still learning. I admittedly had no one closer to me than Eddie, and probably never would. Our friendship went back nearly fifteen years and I was no longer the kind of person willing to invest that much time in constructing another bridge. Our connection, however, was not built on level ground. Intellectually he was far my superior. His knowledge flirted heavily with any historical or pop-cultural topic you could imagine, and his charisma and charm were immeasurable. More than just my friend, Eddie was the only one in the world so linked to my child mind. I respected him immensely and loved him without flinching, even when in the depths of the maddening hell summoned by the terminal sickness of his father. As far as I could tell, his otherworldly insight into the faults of those around him never pertained to me, nor did his flawlessly instinctual judgments of character. His enthusiasm for me particularly, and to a lesser extent our small circle of friends, was never betrayed as it was for most of those unlucky enough to find themselves on the fringe peering in. Eddie and I had probably been drunk together more often than we were sober, but there was a glory in our breed of drunkenness that put us apart from the locals that crammed themselves into the same dusty bar night after night. It slurred our speech but exacted our vision. We were surely to be plucked from our exhausting but noble journey around the familiar track of our small town and reassigned to an alien ocean of a life more profound. We weren't like them, we told ourselves. We mattered.

So in this brief hiatus between tours, the fact that there was no compulsion to walk out the door and accompany him at the bar where we had spent most of our adult lives confounded me as any new knowledge would. He was an old hero of mine, one I had long ago been given in exchange for a different version of myself, so the charge from him to me had always been deep and essential whether I was willing to admit it or not. But something now was nagging me to step back, to accept our spaces, and cherish the pause between frantic gulps of lifeblood. Maybe, as I had once thought while looking at my parents across the dinner table before I began down my own road, I could love him and simultaneously need him no longer. Maybe, but that conclusion was a terrifying one and I was not willing to accept it so easily. As if snapped from a dream, I resumed life as myself and quickly veered back onto the path I had always tread. There was an addictive danger outside and so, with all its flare and speed, the undisputed champion of this new internal bout was still *desire*—my desire for other people and for the attention they gave me and the comfort in our commonalities and in the safety that herd provided. I put the guitar down and quietly left my house, taking extra care not to wake Hannah who was sleeping alone in the bedroom upstairs. It was raining gently. I inhaled the shiny old air and though my mind raced, my betrayed heart thudded heavy. I made the same right turn out my front door and headed up the same hill toward the bar, struggling with each step that I took away from the massive, immovable center.

With an inspired enthusiasm wrested from an uninspired contentment, Eddie and I thwarted fate that night—as we had always done—by drunkenly reveling in our tales of atavistic conquests, feverishly assembling fortifications around our holy past in order to protect it from the oncoming dawn and its dangerous change. When together, we were suspended in brilliance; feral children, full of blind faith in glorious things. We drank and spoke to shadows and we laughed in voices not yet made tired by protest or sadness. We celebrated false a victory as we once had in the sixth grade when a bunch of us cornered a neighborhood kid named Daniel Whitfield in a street hockey game and ripped his dirty shirt off his body into pieces while laughing at the efficiency of our hybrid monster (though unbeknownst to Eddie and the others that joined us in our unprovoked tirade, I had returned to Daniel's house the next afternoon and plaintively handed him my entire week's allowance so that he might buy another shirt and begged his forgiveness as I wept for him and for the terrible pain the whole world would surely cause us). Eddie and I took our places under a spell we remembered fondly, one that shielded us from the itch sober men developed that foolishly leads them to gamble with a future that could bring new beauty as easily as it could death or failure. As aging men, we encountered our unfair present and uncertain futures, and we took a drink as if it were a cautious step backward before scampering behind the motherly leg of our pasts. Here, at Father Baker's, we were hopelessly locked in a sacred intoxicated gaze with youth, and in its eyes we saw mutual simplicity. Here Eddie was not a high school teacher and I was not a musician, because our identities were drowned in the flood of the happiness we disingenuously told ourselves would last forever. If we broke from our huddle, we would find nothing but loneliness in the dark woods and there was nothing more horrific than that.

At 2:30 the next morning I stumbled through my door and slunk into the bed next to Hannah, failing miserably at trying not to wake her.

"Shhh sizzz jussa dream yer still dreaming shhhh," I mumbled as I pulled the blanket up over my chest.

"Honey, you smell like a hobo," she laughed groggily. "Where were you? I was lonely."

"Me'en Eddie had one drink."

"One? That glass must have been a hundred feet tall. Why didn't you tell me? I would have gone with you."

"It's all-dudes-no-chicks," I said as I turned my back to her in order to hide potential faint traces of perfume. I felt her sit up on her elbow as she spoke closer into my ear, her freshly washed hair cascading down the front of my neck.

"Can it be one-dude-one-chick soon? We haven't had a date in so long."

"I know, I promise."

"You promise what?"

"I promise someday."

At this, she withdrew quickly and put her back to mine, frustrated that someday was all I could offer her. But the sad truth was that someday was all I had. After all these years, I still knew not what I could give her—and I still knew not when.

CHAPTER EIGHT

AJURY OF ADMINISTRATORS VOTED IN favor of my guilt. I wasn't present. I learned that Laura was never even contacted concerning the matter in the first place, so she wasn't present either. This example of Virginia Tech's ineptitude in relating to or communicating with their student body was second in audacity only to the early September death of a sophomore whose body was found in the bushes after falling from the tenth floor of her dorm building. Me and two of my friends had unknowingly walked past her on our way to a party as she lay mangled but hidden a few feet from the sidewalk. The next morning when she was discovered, the president made no mention of it, and when asked, teachers were "instructed not to comment." Some said that it was an accident, that she rolled from her top bunk directly out the window, which was not likely but, given the set up of the dorm rooms, definitely possible. Rather than claim responsibility for faulty design, VT's stance would be to call it an "unintentional" suicide, which sent her poor family into an emotional tailspin. There were no therapy sessions set up for her friends, no on campus vigil, and her roommate was given a 4.0 and sent home for the remainder of the semester where she could stay quiet. So, when I called my father to let him know that

I had received a letter which outlined the results of a clandestine meeting and which politely asked me to either resign and take zero credits or stay and receive a 0.0 grade average and complete 300 hours of community service, he was not surprised.

"That school needs to get its shit together and learn how to talk to its students instead of keeping them in the dark. Fuck 'em. Just come home. I know how much you hate the idea, but you can at least finish the semester here." I was on a plane the next evening and was enrolled in Ithaca College by the end of the week. I didn't look back at VT until almost a decade later when the entire world was forced to gaze somberly upon it and collectively wonder with tears in its eyes how chaos of such an ungodly magnitude could befall so many innocent, unsuspecting people. My father and I, sad and sick with anger, needn't ask.

CHAPTER NINE

WHEN AUGUST ARRIVED, AND I FELT well enough to take the stage again, it was only Chet and Cube and I in the bus now that Frank had informally resigned or been dishonorably discharged, depending on how you looked at it—if you chose to actually look at it at all, which none of us really did. Cube was my tour manager, which meant he ran my entire life on the road, handling all things related to money and time. It also meant he was subjected hourly to a level of stress that has made men of less patience abandon their obligation to sanity and discover God. Cube earned his nickname because he was as tall as he was wide as he was deep—six-foot-six, and easily 280 pounds, with thick black glasses in front of his beady eyes and under his tilted flat-brimmed black snapback upon which was embroidered a different word seemingly every time I encountered him. Cube had been the doorman at a bar Frank and Evan and I frequented in our late teens and given how often we drank there, the four of us became friends through lack of other company. He was covered in tattoos, loved to fight, had a small dog, and when he laughed—which was often—he laughed willingly, convincingly, and deeply. He was also an encyclopedia of music trivia. On busy nights, I would stand at the door with him and help check IDs while he talked to me about his dreams of moving to San Francisco. On slow ones, he would sit at the bar with us and suck down beer as if he wasn't even on the clock. When I decided that things on the road were happening too quickly and too often for me and Frank alone to properly attend to, Cube was the first person I called to help me handle all the responsibilities. After much convincing, he quit his job as the bar's gatekeeper to start a life taking care of us on the road. Cube had a Zen-like calm to him most of the time, but could be, if prompted, responsible for absolutely stunning acts of violence. Once in Fort Wayne, Indiana I saw him grab a mouthy drunk by his collar and punch him so hard in the face that the poor man exploded out of the back of his own shirt like he had been spring-loaded inside of it and fell back against the bar, topless and flabby. Cube then calmly used the shirt to wipe up the beer that had spilled and went back to slowly sipping his refreshing Jack and Coke next to me while the entire place stood with their jaws agape.

In stark opposition to my responsible tour manager, Chet— my sound engineer—gave me the impression that he burst into existence out of a timeless void as a fully-formed monstrosity in an upstate swampland with a cigarette in his mouth clutching half a tallboy of warm cheap beer. He was not the kind of person that you can imagine as an innocently curious young child doing things that normal children do in their early development like making friends, kissing girls, playing sports, or not putting their dicks in ant hills for money. Chet was a specimen, a ruthless and unrelenting explosion of senses. He desired more pleasure than joy and required more touching than feeling. I could discreetly observe him for hours and each moment would be more fascinating than the last. His brown hair was short and perpetually mussed, his eyes were enormous and bloodshot, his teeth were stained yellow, and he was speckled with horrible tattoos, but he was, despite all his mental instability, a remarkable sound technician. I had already begun touring when we met at a mutual friends house over a heaping pile of drugs after Father Baker's last call, but when I told him, through clenched teeth, that I could really use a professional sound engineer on tour, it was serendipitously revealed that Chet moonlighted as the house sound guy at a biker bar in the suburbs and he lunged at the chance to tour with me full time. I liked to think it was a selfless act of kindness, but I knew as well as he did that beyond the confines of our small city there were prettier women to fuck and better drugs to ingest. Despite never really vibing with Frank, he had been with me at every show since that cold, blue early morning.

Chet was young, rich, full of life, known by absolutely everyone in town, and hopelessly addicted to sensations. He seemed larger than life, something that was there instead of is here, a distant display of fireworks that I could only watch in awe from the outside—to get too close meant changing the view into something less sublime and far more dangerous. In spite of his almost inhuman amount of drug intake, Chet had the sharpest memory of anyone I had ever encountered and was able to see the minutia of entire events with astounding clarity. More than just recalling details, he had a way of telling stories as if he folded time upon itself to allow us instantaneous access to the past. One was not just reminded, one was repeatedly made present. The remarkable thing about it, though, was that his stories were never the centerpiece of his table, but instead powerful anecdotes revealed casually like aces from up a sleeve. Once, upon passing a homeless man on the streets of Chicago, he was reminded of the time he took a paraplegic Vietnam veteran home with him and found him on the couch the next morning covered in piss, unable to move without the wheelchair that Chet had forgotten to retrieve from the car after carrying the man up the stairs to his apartment and passing out on the floor of his bedroom. Having Chet there was like having your own Hunter S. Thompson, a poetic secretary who had access to every file under the sun but I was convinced that at any moment he could pop out of existence the same way he popped in, appearing suddenly in the bogs of a distant planet where he would shriek as his lungs adapted to whatever element served as air, and either start masturbating or looking for drugs or both.

There was a palpable excitability from the moment the tour bus picked us up from my house where we had all been waiting. The upcoming tour promised to be the best American tour I had done yet, so my manager decided it was finally time I afforded myself and my small crew some comfort not typically found in our van. If I chose to look at the enthusiasm from a distance I could easily say that it was due to the perks that a tour bus provided—none of us would ever be responsible for driving, and we would be able to sleep soundly in private bunks. However, if laid on the glass under a microscope, Frank's absence was undeniably the source of such joy.

An inconsiderate awkwardness had been deflated, and from our forced position against the absolute limit of our collective emotional parameters, we were finally given relief from his imposing presence and allowed to settle back to a comfort level we knew a long time ago. We had more breath to laugh with, more room in which to open our arms and accept possibility, more distance with which to see things fully and as they were. We adorned ourselves in the colors we had kept secret.

Without Frank, I was required to tune my own guitar, set up my own amp, and remember to get my own beer, which wasn't too hard given that I was a fully functioning adult. But, like an old book, it did require a rediscovering and dusting off. In Cleveland on the very first night, I had forgotten that a few songs in the middle of my set were in a different tuning, and rather than quickly changing out to a pre-tuned back-up I was left making small talk while I rushed to tune the one I had already been playing then put it back to where it began six songs later in order to finish the set in the original tuning. I was terrified of small talk, and, admittedly, no good at it, but the only thing I feared more than speaking to an audience was a pregnant pause, particularly the kind authored by a room full of hardworking people, which will swell and ache and will threaten to burst into innumerable angry pieces in a blinding flurry that rattles even the stately truth of your reputation, if not punctured gently and decompressed by a poignant story or a quick return to the paid-for entertainment. Allowing a silence is issuing a challenge to a crowd's obedience, and if one has not enamored or intrigued every single person who sets their eyes upon them, the challenge will be met with disdain. In the one second it takes a drunk audience member to realize that he—more than you or anyone else—has the floor, the disapproval will ring like church bells across a low-lying vale and you will have lost them to their own uproar. As a musician, you very rarely come back from that. I had seen it happen on numerous occasions to other acts and it has happened to me only once when, in a drunken stupor, I began playing and singing two different songs and could not for the life of me figure out which half was correct—but sense and intelligence very rarely ever make it past the fourth glass. I checked the setlist three or four times, retuned my guitar, took a swig of beer, and immediately made the exact same mistake. The crowd, understanding that they were not going to get their money's worth, began to speak loudly and turn away from the stage, back to their own private affairs, which sobered me up to the point that I could have flown a commercial jet through a storm and sent me on a downward spiral of self-loathing and regret right there on the ten-foot by twelve-foot wooden stage in a Sacramento bar. From that moment, I vowed to fear the pause and never ever again assume I was good enough to make people fall in love so willingly.

If Frank had been there in Cleveland that night, he would have had three guitars polished, tuned, and restrung hours before my set time, and what pained me about knowing that, was not that he was gone, but having to admit to myself that I actually needed him. In Philadelphia a few nights later, I had forgotten to take water onstage. Rather than continue, I decided I was in no state to hit the note on the approaching horizon and stopped the song.

"Shit," I said, dropping my guitar to my side. "I hate to do this to you all, but I really need a fucking drink." I heard some people laugh awkwardly and whisper.

"Bartender? Can you pass me up a beer? I'm good for it." After a few seconds a cold bottle was extended out to me from beyond the lights that shined from the ceiling like a ladder coming to rescue me from the flames.

"Thank you kindly," I said, and took a long, purposeful swig. I began the song again. "This song—once again—is called 'Morning Moon.'"

CHAPTER TEN

RETURNING TO MY PARENTS' HOUSE required no pardon or ceremony. I quietly reinhabited the tiny room at the end of the upstairs hallway and effortlessly resumed moping around idly while my mother swaddled me with an undaunted love that operated independently of my use for it, like a light bulb glowing warmly in a long-abandoned office. It was the most unremarkable room you could imagine, but at one point I was far more concerned with what was outside of it than what its walls held in, walls which were undecorated and painted the same dull color as the carpet. There was a small closet where my parents had begun to store their winter coats and shoes and old records and a wooden dresser against the wall opposite the bed. Atop that dresser was an old record player my father bought from the flea market. Then there was the window at the foot of my bed that overlooked the backyard, the window that had provided all the ornamentation I ever needed growing up. In the winter I could see clear across the lawn into our backyard neighbor's kitchen window, but for nine months straight, the enormous leaves of a Water Maple, one whose folds and protrusions I came to know intimately as a child, often sneaking into it from my window as if into the arms of someone entirely forbidden to me, shielded me from the view of the beneath and around, open only to that which was above. I would lay in its cradle perfectly balanced under a tent of stars looking at the dirty magazines I found in the woods and feel as if its thick branches and my thin spine were coextensive, vaulting my own being both deep into the soil of the earth in one direction and out toward the boastful unknown in the other. It was almost winter now, and though I was an adult and needn't worry about hiding myself amidst its leaves from the prying eyes of neighbors at dinner, climbing into the tree didn't feel right unless it felt secretive.

I was unworthy of my parents' tenderness. My attempt at breaking out of the suburban cell was not only a failure, it was an insult to the people that raised me selflessly and a humiliating exhibition of my weakness to the friends whose respect I had so hungrily sought. I had ventured to seek my own meal, and rather than nobly starve to death on foreign ground when I had lost the scent of destiny, I fearfully scurried back to the womb where every want and need was provided in abundance by perfect biology. Though this setup might sound ideal to the lazy or confused, I hadn't intended to be either. Knowing that my only purpose now was to float vulnerably while awaiting factors beyond my control or understanding to decide on the specific conditions of my new dawn irritated every anxious cell in my body. The natural ease with which I had endured my family's structure and rituals was no longer available to me. I felt burdensome. I was simultaneously anchored in the comfort of the ordinary and tied to the lofty absurd, yet incapable of fully committing my soul to either. The ceilings had lowered and the sunlight that seeped through the windows was custom contoured to fall warmly upon only those who belonged there while I, on the other hand, was forced to plod through it awkwardly, all the while begging for something that wasn't rightfully mine to be shared with me at another's expense.

The mood felt like an oversized suit. I was an unsightly remainder tacked onto the end of a gorgeous equation. No longer a resident of the house, I was a tenant who couldn't afford rent. The sky above me was clouded. No transmissions reached me. My guitar lay silent in its case near my bed and I stared at it, envious of its ability to just be a guitar that could so comfortably lay silent in its case.

With most of my neighborhood acquaintances away at school—and luckily for me, Hannah, whom I could not possibly face while in such a lowly, shameful state—I found myself spending a majority of my time with Eddie and Aaron, neither of them having any reason to move out of their parents' homes after graduation. I had known Eddie Reilly since I was little. We lived relatively close to each other our whole young lives, and when all the neighborhood kids would gather for street hockey games, I would stand off to the side and laugh with the others at the impressions he did but I only began hanging out with him intimately in the tenth grade after he saw me with a comic book in study hall and asked if I had read something called *On The Road*—which I hadn't even heard of. The next day he found me at my locker and lent me his copy. By the end of the day, after I had passionately devoured the entire seedy account of drugs and life and lust like the first meal after a fast, what was once only ambient brightness now began to take form and I could suddenly determine from which direction light came.

From that day on I desperately sought Eddie's approval, a reward he withheld from me like an older brother with a lewd secret. Though initially I was cautious of him because he was loud and seemed more dangerous than children our age should be, the energy he radiated was undeniable and I found myself drawn to him like one was drawn to music that called out from the open door of a church on a dark street.

Eddie had refused to apply to any college, calling it "nutrient deficient bullshit," a move that made perfect sense to those who knew him given his preternatural ability to retain and apply any information he came across in almost any field you could imagine. Growing up, Eddie drank beer once in a while, looked cool as hell smoking a cigarette, and absorbed knowledge like a root took in water. He thought and spoke like the writers I had begun emulating, but rarely had I ever seen him pick up a pen, despite my constant urgings for him to create something I could consume. I was eager for the gifts he withheld. His genius was the first thing I saw with the eye of my heart. I wanted him to make something that only we could give to the world, something odd that would forever owe us its life and keep us bound to each other long after we were able to make anything at all. Unfortunately, Eddie's priority was stealing his old man's alcohol and talking in circles about his difficulty accepting the notion of God. As a sixteen-year-old, I didn't understand how God could not exist when proof of him seemed present in everything lovely, peculiar and immense, which was, to me, everything there was, but I listened closely because I wanted Eddie to feel that no one else understood him like I did, that together we had access to a depth of thought that eluded our peers and set us apart from them, that our discussions about death and God and hell and hope were an elite secret language and every effortless hour that passed in each others' company was a landmark that assured me of my path onward through the overgrowth of teen angst and confusion toward my brand new destiny as a humble scribe of a hyper life. Deep down, however, I knew that he would talk no matter who listened, and that I didn't uniquely matter to him at all. I was just a body that filled some of the Godless open space he feared more than hell itself.

Eddie was the first to get his driver's license and once it was acquired we would take frequent trips to the city in his father's car to drive around aimlessly, marveling at people we hadn't ever seen. One afternoon, however, Eddie decided to stop at an old independent record store that we had often thoughtlessly passed called *Home Of The Hits*. This was a misnomer since, for the first ten minutes of perusing the cassettes, I could not find anything that had ever been on the radio, but when I came upon a tape by some band called Bad Religion, I was so intrigued by the art on the cover that I spent half of my week's allowance without a second thought and my viewing angle was forever widened on a whim. The image registered on a purely spiritual level, one that evaded the language of cognition, but the music itself—once we put it into the cassette player of the car—was so unpolished, intimate, unpredictable, and profane that I could not help but expose all nerves to it and ride a swelling wave upward toward a new perception of music as a whole. It was nothing like the gentle arrangement of recognizable sounds my father had always played for me, which meant that this band was not one I equated with the comfort of his home and therefore their songs became more than just songs. They were a rebellion. Purchasing *Suffer* was a spontaneous, irrational reaction to nothing more than an illustration, but the sounds that the image represented not only yanked me out of the safety of my parents' music room, it boarded it up behind me. Of course I would eventually have to explain to them what happened to all my money when I inevitably needed more, but I was unconcerned with that distant future because in that impeccable series of moments there was nothing more than me and Eddie and a car with the windows down and music that was loud and weird and beautiful and that future of explanations didn't exist on a plane I could ever inhabit again. Anything that wasn't now wasn't at all and all that was could not be otherwise. On that day I had no reason to be alive other than to surrender to a raw, haunting energy and the new wavelengths of radiation that it made visible. On that day music made the world, not the other way around. On that day I was young and still had a taste of the holy on my lips.

Like me and Eddie, Aaron Doyle also lived with his parents, but unlike me and Eddie, he attended the community college. I met Aaron in sixth grade at a birthday party thrown by a kid on our street, and while we stood in the back yard drinking pop pretending it was beer Aaron told me a story about putting his finger inside of a girl behind the school. It couldn't be true. You needed to be a doctor to put a part of your body into the body of another human being. There was simply no chance that I would so casually be shown such a superbly awful, lurid corner of my own familiar boyhood without some sort of consideration for my safety. One does not simply blurt out that he ventured inside another human body without warning—and if he does, he does not use the beautiful human language that, until then, had only been used in my life to espouse love and extol sacred things.

My throat tightened and a dour evil came over the land. I felt like I had lost my mother in a city-sized grocery store. As I stared at Aaron in horror, he just laughed and wiggled his middle finger in a recreation to that particular evening's events. Tears welled up in my eyes. I scanned the yard, looking for something to focus on—anything other than the filthy, intrusive weapon he let squirm in my face—but all I could see were the girls I dreamt about loving and kissing and holding hands with now split violently open, their insides exposed to the angry boys circling them in the grass like sharks in the water. And I began to weep. My mother had been fingered. My god. My small body couldn't take it. I retreated to a hedge against the fence in a dark corner of the yard and cried as I stared at the mental image of my future girlfriends and wives, eviscerated by giggling men. There was blood everywhere. Everyone I knew had begun dying at the same time.

That night, driven completely mad by his sordid tale of lust, I went home and did the only thing left to do: I boldly accepted a new reality in which girls were fingered and I may be called upon to be their fingerer. With extreme caution I placed that ugly, misshapen fact on the shelf in the perfect white room that stored all I remembered about divinity and began practicing for the awful day of imminent death by pushing my fingertip in and out of my bellybutton. When I finally fell asleep I dreamt that I was floating in space, looking back sorrowfully at a distant earth that was neither big nor blue nor round.

CHAPTER ELEVEN

MY THIRD RECORD WAS SCHEDULED TO come out later that month on the day of my Los Angeles show. In preparation for what would be an unsolicited assault of overprivileged, uninformed, and generally nasty opinions from online bloggers and critics, I spent a majority of my time on the bus in a hypnotic state bolstering my sense of self, which I intended to make bulletproof and unwavering. When I wasn't doing an interview for a bullshit online zine that nobody would ever read or taking photos for an amateur online journal that would never get published, I was busily building my defenses. My headphones were glued into my ears and through them came that familiar, nurturing disembodied voice I had come to accept as that of God itself and nothing could inspire me like his kind validations. I had basically memorized the sermon so that, even when doing other activities, it rolled around in the back of my head like a mantra.

"Welcome to Mind Magic," it said. "You are worthy of your life." That's how it always began—a reaffirmation that, no matter what anyone said, I was something different and unique and special. There were certain tapes I would listen to when I was awake in order to help me walk calmly through tempestuous situations, and others that I was only supposed to listen to when asleep, ones that held at bay my meaningless, nonsensical dreams, and replaced them with focused promotions of my self-worth. And when I did so, I would wake up feeling invincible. If anyone had known of such juvenile means of gaining inner strength, they probably would have dismissed it without a second thought, but those people hadn't paid the fifteen hundred dollars that I had, so I couldn't expect them to understand the complex workings of a new school of thought operating on an enlightened level of the human mind. Positive thinking was a foreign term in this industry, particularly when you had made an entire career around an image of a nihilistic alcoholic like I had, but it became more and more obvious to me that my drinking and drink-related vices (which were all of them), were spawned not out of want or need but out of a blind adherence to some inescapable laws of a ritualistic sacrifice and a suffocating fear of losing the love of people who expected more misery than I was capable of cultivating while sober. I could not think of another profession in which someone offers you poison as a thank you for the wonderful things you do while alive.

When I got involved in the music scene playing open mic nights at small bars, I found it liberating to have my innately self-destructive tendencies heralded. There was no greater feeling in the world than discovering a place where secret shame was greeted enthusiastically and dysfunctions were praised. Eventually, as I began to travel more, I was so free that I found myself growing bored with the things most men deemed exquisite and I was forced to step up by crawling further down.

But *If I was alive, why not feel like it?* My senses exploded every minute of every night for those first few years of touring. There was not a drink, drug, fight, or woman that I would turn down if offered, no shameful deed that I would not deny if questioned, no insult that I would suffer, no regrets that I could carry and for a while it seemed that I was not only willing to die for my music, but secretly trying to. I was an unabashed pleasure-monger through and through, a hunter that took the stage pursing a different kill through dangerous new terrain each night, and Frank only fueled that fire. Life was so good back then that I almost took relief in knowing I would be dead long before I was incapable of living it. I had a maniacal ambition, and was both brazenly unaware of others and entirely full of my self. These key qualities, plus a few enablers on each shoulder, made for a condition of nature that weeded out the weaker human beings who were trapped here on earth because they could not squint into the piercing radiance of inebriation and music like I so easily could. The ones who instead turned away to look clearly upon nothing extraordinary.

CHAPTER TWELVE

AARON'S PARENTS ALWAYS THREW extravagant Christmas parties. His father was a wealthy architect so their house was enormous and they would spare no expense providing a spectacle for anyone who wished to walk through their door and stand in admiration. There was a piano player and an open bar and a tree that reached twenty feet high and new cars with big bows on them in the driveway every other year. It was a ritual that had gone on since I met Aaron, and as fun as it always was for me, I imagined it was a source of tremendous discomfort for my parents who would have to drop me off in front of a house that looked like it belonged in The Hamptons before returning to their modest home and wrapping far more thoughtful but less exciting presents.

That year, however, I was apprehensive because I knew I would be interviewed about Virginia Tech and presumably forced to listen to stories about the college life that should have been mine told by old friends who really no longer were. In preparation, I had voraciously practiced my conversations as if they were State of the Union addresses and felt confident that I had an answer for any question and a rebuttal for any remark, sometimes even thinking so far ahead as to counter their rejoinder with one of many possible retorts of my own. As this imaginary inquisition progressed, the prepared responses lent themselves to a varied array of secondary and tertiary questions, all which I had invented in advance and which I felt ready to field with poise. In total, there were over seventeen million possible conversations that could occur between me and any number of guests lasting any amount of time in any order and I was certain I had envisioned them all.

Because both of us planned on drinking, Eddie and I had my mom drop us off around 7:00 p.m. We were lovingly told to call for pick up no later than midnight. After that, it would be up to us to find our own ride. When we arrived, Eddie entered the carnival as if he were a veteran clown while I went in almost completely unnoticed behind him in his shadow, as was typically the case. He marched stridently into the room and as I shuffled to get the snow off of my shoes, Aaron's already gleefully drunk father came over to hug me. It was then that something curious happened. As my head rested on his shoulder for no longer than a few seconds and I was able to scan the room without obstruction, a darkness fell upon me that was simultaneously a sense of déjà vu and an intense, cerebral fear of something unknown. Had I dreamt of my death in this room on this night? Had I dreamt of someone else's? My stomach twisted in the same manner it had when I was told I was under suspicion of cheating and my vision blurred around the periphery. I had been there before, not at a previous Christmas party at Aaron's house but at that same exact present moment. I knew it. My brain registered it as an indisputable fact, which was surprising considering how impossible it was. Yet, there it was. I was returning to something intimately familiar—maybe not in this body but at this exact precipice with the exact same wind at my back. Then, after what felt like centuries, he loosened his embrace and the dread vanished.

Shoes, coat, and hat now removed, I spotted Aaron near the stairs having an animated conversation with someone I did not recognize and, though the house was filled with people I should have probably exchanged pleasantries with, I was urged to firstly speak to him. In a fashion that was very unlike me, I hurried past Aaron's mother and some old classmates who were all laughing hysterically at something Eddie had said, though what it was genuinely did not concern me. There was a determination in my heart to hit my mark on the floor directly next to Aaron before time ran out. When I finally arrived at his side, I breathed deep and locked into place.

"Ray!" he said excitedly. "Your ears must have been ringing. This is my buddy Frank Qynn."

Aaron held out his hand as if he were showing me to the door.

"Frank goes to school with me. Frank, this is the guy I was just telling you about."

Frank was about a half a foot taller than me with tousled reddish brown hair and smooth, milky-white skin. He was wearing a fedora on the crown of his head, a loosely hanging shirt that draped lazily over his stocky upper body, a necklace with a nondescript key hanging from it, black jeans, and boots. His eyes were dark and his lips were thin. Frank put his hand out unenthusiastically and, when I slid mine forward to meet it, I was overtaken by a voice that sounded like mine but didn't speak the words that my brain would typically supply when encountering a complete stranger.

"Gotta work on that handshake," I said with a half smile. Aaron seemed confused by my attempt at a joke. Frank scratched at his stubbly beard and looked into me, past my eyes.

"What do you mean?" his tone tacitly aggressive.

"No, it's just..." I laughed nervously, confused by my own offensive utterance, though truthfully, I was a bit surprised at how flaccid it was considering his obvious strength. Frank grew visibly agitated and he took a step back, squinting his black eyes; eyes that conveyed to me a timeless primordial strength in the presence of which I was absolutely powerless, one which his weak handshake belied. He seemed irritated beyond reason. I looked around for something reassuring, but there was nothing. Humorless emptiness. He did not find even a modicum of amusement in what I had said and I began to panic.

"I'm just kidding. Forget it."

"Was that, like, a jab or something?" he asked, shifting his weight onto his other leg and crossing his arms. At that point in my life I hadn't ever been in a fight before, but my instincts told me that this was what one looked like just seconds before it began. He didn't like me. As he was bigger than me both in height and strength I knew I didn't stand a chance if things escalated to the point of throwing punches. My heart raced and my throat tightened.

"No," I said, my voice trembling slightly. The air that hovered over us descended further still. I squirmed, looking to Aaron for some sort of help. It was obvious there was something dark and dangerous occurring. "I didn't mean anything by it. Aaron, please explain to him that I was just messing around."

"Well, Raymond. It was a weird thing for you to say."

"What?!" I laughed, incredulously. Suddenly I was alone. "Aaron. Come on. Please. I was kidding with him." Sensing my desperation and vulnerability, Frank inched forward, causing me to take a few steps back as if relinquishing bits of territory that he rightfully deserved.

"Okay…" Aaron said putting his hand on Franks chest as if truncating Franks unspoken inner urge to lash out and hit me, "that will do, Frank. He didn't mean anything by it and he's very sorry. Ray is not known for his comedic timing."

I shook my head, my eyes cast woefully on my own feet.

"Let's go out back and smoke. Calm our nerves a little bit."

I looked up at Frank more desperate for an approval than I had ever remembered being.

He shrugged. "Sure. Yeah. Let's do that."

With this simple indifferent gesture my world refilled with light. I was alive again. The grip that squeezed the breath out of my body and threatened to crunch my bones into a powder loosened and I regained my consciousness, breathing deeply and fully. I had been snatched from certain death by his king-like pardon and I would be forever in his debt. I didn't even smoke weed—a fact that became obvious the first time the joint was passed to me as we stood out on Aaron's back porch talking about music and I fell into a coughing fit—but that wasn't important. What mattered is that I was safe now, both *from* Frank and *with* Frank.

The party transformed peacefully and with great ease into a fantastic celebration of life. I was elated in the company of my friends and relieved to not have to rely on a single one of my practiced conversations about Virginia Tech, even though I did regret wasting all that time spent in preparation sharpening a tool that would never be used. Outside, the snow fell steadily, making it the first white Christmas we had had in almost three years. The alcohol settled into us with beautiful intentions and spread elegantly through our teenage brains, lighting candles as it went. Eddie was in perfect form, impervious to the curious looks from Frank, looks intended to defend Frank from the sacred power of our laughter and love for each other, a love he could not partake in. There was nowhere else to go from here except back to where we began and it felt miraculous.

At around 11:30, the crowd began to break up. No one was willing to offer us a lift home with the snow falling as hard as it was so I finished my beer and stumbled to the phone to wake my mother. After she groggily agreed to brave the storm to save us, I turned around and found two Franks standing behind me. Their eyes were determined. My muscles coiled up and my teeth rattled with nervousness.

"Apologize to me. Right fucking now," they said calmly and quietly so as to not draw attention.

"Really?" I looked down and saw a clenched fist and it occurred to me that they were fully prepared for violence. "I thought we were cool?"

"We were cool. But now you owe me an apology. You humiliated me. After I get what I deserve from you, we can be cool again." I looked around the room, wondering if anyone else was witnessing the strange confrontation taking place, but Eddie and the remaining party guests were oblivious, chatting and laughing and not fearing death while I stood at the brink of a limitless dark wilderness, possessed by an unholy fright. In a few seconds I would be completely out of earshot, stuck at the dead end of a black street with red houses and I would never be able to hear my friends calling out to me from the places the sun fell upon. I was outnumbered. The Franks and I were alone on a distant planet.

"Okay, man. Let's calm down. I'm really sorry about before," I said as if reasoning with men who had guns drawn. "I was joking around with you like you were an old friend, but we don't know each other that well yet. It was super super super uncalled for. I'm, I'm sorry."

"Yes. You are sorry, Raymond. Don't ever forget that."

They put out their hands. "As long as you are sorry, we're cool."

In disbelief, I gripped the one somewhere to the right of the middle and resigned as he moved mine through the thick air.

"And clean yourself up, man. It's embarrassing," he said, pointing to a spot on my shirt. When I looked down at it he flicked my nose hard like a grade-school bully. Then he turned and went back to my group of friends, leaving me standing there alone, hiccupping, in otherwise-silent disbelief.

That night as I began to fall into sleep in the darkness of my bedroom, a buzzing arose in my ears. It was quiet and incredibly pleasant at first, but it became more shrill with each lucid step I took toward dreaming until it had almost overtaken me, shrieking now like a murder of crows. It was warm and smooth and louder than thunder and I was floating inside of it, still aware, like a yolk in a gelatinous field of sound and energy. Every vibration of every molecule in my body was amplified directly against my eardrums. I couldn't hold a thought. As it intensified, my eyes retreated to a distance from which I thought they might never return. The strain this put on them was immense. My head pulsated and I became aware that I was trapped underneath or inside of something indefinable. It was a feeling of extreme claustrophobia under a wide open sky. I panicked. My lungs stopped working. In fact, all pieces of myself conspired against whoever was laying in that bed. I tried to open my eyes but they wouldn't move. They weren't mine. My body had gone to sleep without me. I attempted to move my arm but it was as good as a draft of air attempting to move a mountain. I tried to scream but was unable. I was ghost-like, cleaved into two. Within myself and without myself—formlessly bound by skin and bone to bed and earth. My body was as big as the world and I was something else inside of it, gazing in despair at the cavernous space between the awareness of who I was down here and the flesh that was given access to the stimulus of the room above and around me. I tried again to move, this time focusing harder on my left leg. If I could shift it, my brain might recognize the intrusion of the material realm and awaken to me. It began to work. My leg lifted slightly and dropped but the motion was not enough to wake Raymond who was sleeping soundly in my bed. He needed something louder. Concentrating all of my will onto the muscles and tissues and fibers of my leg so intensely that I actually unified with it, I picked it up again and in midair shifted it so that it came down off the mattress and against the frame with enough force to startle life back into that slumbering husk. I instantly rejoined Raymond and we shot up as if pulled from a dark, cold lake, filling our lungs with as much air as they could hold. The light of the moon that fell across the top half my bed as I sat there was blinding. I felt like I had just been released from an imprisonment in a cave, one in which I suffered while an impostor was loose upon the world relating to and interacting with *my* reality. I looked frantically around me and named out loud the things I saw, bringing them back into my understanding in a feeble attempt to reassemble the straw house that had just been blown in. Across from my bed there were some pictures. Those pictures represented things that I loved. Love was real. I was awake. After two more occasions like this within the same month, I would be diagnosed with sleep apnea.

CHAPTER THIRTEEN

ON A SATURDAY IN AUGUST, ABOUT fourteen days into the tour, Elegy held a record release party in the Foundation Room at the House of Blues in Los Angeles after a sold out matinee show. The entire day was to be a celebration of my latest accomplishment—a ten-song album called *Cease From Troubling* that everyone on my team felt was going be the one to propel me into the stratosphere of indie-rock stardom. Formal, wedding-type invitations had gone out to people I had never seen before or interacted with, but I had been making a concerted effort to put myself in situations that I would normally avoid because I wanted to believe that my therapy was working, so I told myself that it would be alright. That I could manage. Though I still had three months left in which to be refunded if I didn't notice a drastic change in the levels of anxiety that had immobilized me for over a decade, I was hopeful and wanted normality more than I wanted a refund. However, I could not ignore the fact that what I had absorbed inextricably into my sense of self was the primary cause of my drinking, so the effects of reversing a systemic flaw could potentially be further reaching than I had originally understood and quite possibly require me to sober up. This was problematic, as I fucking loved drinking. I loved it because it was the most endearing way to quit the game I was born to lose. I loved it because I still longed for the irrational passion of my youth, the kind that briefly retook possession of me when I was next to Sophia. I loved it because it had taught me the language of my muse. And now I loved it mostly because it erased the shame I felt knowing that I couldn't muster the strength to walk off the world that night in Australia when I had the chance.

If Frank were on tour, I thought as I looked around a surprisingly empty Foundation Room, *he would have arrived early and used his timing as a strike.*

"Nobody else will show up," he would say confidently. I could see the way he spoke it. I could hear his voice. He wasn't there but my mind convinced my body he was and my body reacted accordingly by increasing my heart rate and driving my blood pressure up. My hands began to sweat. I cursed him.

"Fuck you, Frank," I hissed, wounded and mad. His face was bloated with a braggart's pride. He would laugh loudly at my outburst, a hyena-type cackle that reveled in its own blatant insincerity. I could see his ghoulish eyes squinting from underneath his hat. Before the party even began I was undoing myself with his hands.

But for what reason?

I took a step back from myself, surprised at the question that sprung effortlessly from a hidden source. It presented itself without warning in an unprecedented maneuver of spirit. It was a small fist, balled up and hurled awkwardly at the goliath mind. It didn't sting as much as it shocked. It repeated itself.

For what reason are you letting Frank in?

My hands stopped sweating and I could feel my heart slow down. A flash of benevolence brushed passed my furious animal brain. Who cared what Frank thought? He was a sad child who took shelter in the approval of other boring, hateful children.

While he may have vigilantly lorded over the uninspired, I was no longer a soul in his kingdom and I needn't invite him into mine.

For no reason.

I walked over to the bar and ponied up next to Cube and ordered a drink for myself and him. Then I had another. Then one more. By the time Cube and I were on our fourth drink, I had made the executive decision to steer the night comfortably along the same track of deviancy and recidivism that it had always traveled. I could get saved later. No point in disavowing safety just yet.

Eventually people did show up. A lot of people, in fact, and when Chet eventually burst into the room from god knows where—it turned out to be the apartment of a woman he had met at the bar before the show. The woman had a five-year-old son and a husband who was out of town. When the son woke up from a bad dream and walked in on them fucking, Chet, who was entirely under the sheets at that moment began barking like a dog. The child assumed that their dog was in her bed and, having avoided a life-altering trauma, peacefully returned to sleep. I would learn of this a year later—I had already began to feel a lightness in my feet, a feeling that I had come to value more than any other in the world because it was the sum of all the others in the world except it was at once. A bright, numb gasp that elevated you in order to align the pins in a lock you weren't certain you were holding the right key for. It was sharp and concise and always waiting to excitedly share its bounty. I welcomed it and cherished the comfort of its firm grip because it meant the lost and starving spirit that was frantically waving and screaming my name would now be rescued from among a great emptiness and could reassume its rightful place at the source of all the grand things I knew and made. Sobriety was way too impractical. How could I be so selfish as to dash the cup and starve the crowd? This was right. This was the only way.

"If I could bottle this exact feeling I have right now and sell it, I'd make millions," I said to Chet.

"Well, unfortunately for you, but luckily for every other adult, someone already has. They called it alcohol. Anyone here got coke?"

"You *just* walked in the door," I said, feigning shock at his urgency. "I don't know. That guy looks like a creep," I said, pointing to a tall man in a bowtie drinking a margarita, "Go ask him."

"Look, I know you think I have a coke problem but I do not. I can quit any time I run out."

For the next few hours I milled about, drank more, shook some hands, and in fleeting moments of nervous hope, scoured the room for Sophia, though I knew in my heart she wouldn't arrive. She would keep her promise.

"I found the dude," Chet said at around eleven-thirty.

"You're aware that we have to be in Vegas by noon tomorrow, right?

"I know that, dickhead. I am a consummate professional at snorting cocaine." He held the small ziplock bag full of white powder at eye level as if figuring out his next move in Jenga.

"Jesus."

"It's better to have it and not need it than need it and not have it. We're going to a party in the hills. Some girl just invited us. Says she works for your street team, whatever the fuck that is." He dipped a key into the bag and then took the powder off of it with a deep breath in. "The car service will be here in twenty." He dipped the key in again and put it to the other nostril. "Street Team," he snickered. "Little punk rock monkeys running around worshipping you like you're Father Yod. Your life is so fucking asinine."

"Whose house are we going to?" I asked as he held his key under my nose.

"I have no idea."

I inhaled quickly and tipped my head back. "Is it Skrillex?"

Chet put the key to my other nostril. "I said I don't know. Don't ruin this for me."

I inhaled again. "Can I just leave my own party?" Chet laughed.

"You think anyone here but me and Cube actually gives a fuck about you?" He twisted up the baggie and stashed it in the pocket of his blazer. "You're a meal ticket, and there's not a person in this room who wouldn't devour you like one."

"You know you don't actually eat meal tickets right?" Chet disappeared into the crowd without responding, but for the most part he was right. After the obligatory introductions that took place well over four hours prior, not a single person involved with my label attempted a real conversation with me. Come to think of it, nor did anyone working for the radio stations or magazines or websites or merchandise companies or guitar companies. They did, however, drink free alcohol and eat free appetizers and gossip without compunction like the parasites they were. Everyone in that room was worth upward of a million dollars (some certainly more) and a good portion of it was made as a result of my considerable success. So where was the gratitude? Where was the acknowledgment of my sacrifice and hard work? There was not even the slightest attempt at feigning interest in my success anymore. The days of being sprayed with a celebratory beer by Claire and our friends as I walked into our apartment after my first month-long tour were almost too long ago to be recalled. Truthfully, it would be a miracle if Eddie even took the breath to congratulate me as I walked offstage. The Battle of Who-Couldn't-Care-Less had enlisted my friends long ago and as it was currently being waged in homes and bars and offices all across the country, their services were desperately needed. By now the death toll must have been in the billions.

As I looked around the room again I sensed an army approaching. I heard every tattooed, plaid, pearl snap shirt-wearing soldier whistling idly as they sauntered through the rivers of blood that were fed by the open veins of my artistic brethren and I began to fear for my own life. In writing and recording this last album how could I have forgotten to take the steps required to harden my skin? Now I was sinking in doubt. Why hadn't anyone there congratulated me? Why hadn't they told me about the sadness they heard in my voice or how my lyrics resonated within the cavities of their own soul? For a moment I contemplated asking any number of the remaining guests what their favorite song or lyric was, so parched and starving was I. I was also outrageously high on drugs and decided that I needed to get on the internet immediately.

Surely people would be discussing my record on message boards. I had read all the early reviews, but those magazines were on Elegy's payroll and their takes were just disingenuous testimonies meant to push sales and maintain mutually beneficial business relationships. I needed to know what real people thought, the honest ones who made time in their lives to go out and buy the records. The ones who called off work, hired babysitters, borrowed money, and begged for rides in order to come to my shows when I was in their town. In other words, I needed a quick fix of the approval provided by the kind of people that wouldn't be caught dead in the company I was currently in. The ones I truly loved and actually worked for. I hurried outside onto the balcony to get cell phone reception and, as I did, a half dozen backed up texts from my wife came rushing to my phone, which I ignored to pursue the more important matter at hand. Hannah would have to wait.

A Google search of the album title resulted in a few pages of reviews by online bloggers and self-proclaimed authorities on "indie-punk." Frantically scouring the comment sections of different music websites, what I quickly ascertained was that a large portion of my fans liked the album because of the considerable changes I made to my sound, which would have been refreshing except for the fact that an equally large portion hated it because they didn't think I made enough considerable changes to my sound. "Resting on Laurels" was a term that appeared more often than my own name. This wasn't two sides of the same argument, mind you, but rather half of an argument about two separate subjects. I looked around the empty balcony with a righteous indignation.

"These fucking idiots," I said as I shook my head in disbelief. My heart sank. What the fuck was I even doing making music anymore? It would have been one thing to write "I hate it because of all the changes" in response to someone who says "I like it because of all the changes" because that at least acknowledges that change exists and we can then open a dialogue around a consensually agreed upon focal point. But this horse shit? It was just plain wrong. People couldn't even agree on whether or not fundamental change was apparent at all. Were they listening to the same record? Everything went black. I twisted my phone in my hands like I was wringing a wet towel, and as tears of frustration welled up in my eyes, I beat my fist against the side of my head in a short fit of uncontrollable anger with such force I could feel them leap off my face. Anyone with an internet connection was a critic—and as unbelievable as it sounds, their unchecked, uninformed, and often spiteful rants had the power to affect not only my mental health but my financial security. That concept was maddening. I was in the hands of millions, how could I expect them to communicate amongst each other in a common language in order to reach an agreement that they be delicate with a heart I had essentially forced upon them? There were too many improbable factors. It was like trying to reason with a lion that has you cornered.

Years prior, when I began making music, I had stock in knowledge. It was both a trophy and a tool. I was well-read because my parents paid for my education and it made me privileged. I knew things that other people couldn't know because I had been taught by people they hadn't met and I saw things they couldn't ever have seen because I was naive enough to pick up a guitar and follow it. But now what was I worth? The books I discovered at the behest of my intellectually superior professors are now coming to me thanks to an algorithm developed to suggest what I should buy based on what other *similar shoppers* have also bought, and when I gently press a piece of glass, I can have a digital copy delivered instantly to me as I sit on any couch in any room in any country. The band I found after four hours of sifting through records at a music store downtown now has their tenth album funded by their fans available online and doesn't even need to get in a van in order to deliver it to them as long as they have a SoundCloud account open to the public, some of them even willing to exchange it for an imaginary cryptocurrency which operates independently of any central authority. So what was *anything* really worth if it stood naked in the middle of the world and was made available to all forever? An artist looking for his day in the sun would dry up quickly in this new, vast, ruthless, distracted, impersonal desert of meaninglessness and too many people are happy to log in and pick his bones. Why was I hopelessly struggling to cross it? I never disliked humanity more than when I watched how indifferently they reacted to creation.

Chet poked his head outside.

"There you are. The car is downstairs."

"Good. Get me the fuck out of here."

CHAPTER FOURTEEN

IN ORDER TO SAVE ENOUGH MONEY TO MOVE out of my parent's house, I worked in the small nursery my mother managed, but even after a year of saving my paychecks I knew full well I would still need to recruit a roommate or two in order to maintain the five-hundred-dollar monthly rent most landlords seemed to be asking. Without any old friends willing to leave the creature comforts of the suburbs, I had only one true option other than bringing in a complete stranger. Frank.

Truth be told, he and I had grown considerably closer since our initial encounter at Aaron's Christmas party and he had definitely held his promise of being *cool* with me when we found ourselves in the same places, but he tended to put me on edge when drunk and I always carried with me a nagging sense of inferiority in his presence, which developed into a habit of emotionally wincing when he joked with me, his humor seeming to come from a place much darker than my friends. However, he had firmly attached himself to our small circle and I was out of other options. With much hesitation I called him and asked him to be my housemate.

"Absolutely," he said, surprisingly enthusiastic. His response was in stark contrast to the way I had envisioned it going in my head. I couldn't figure this guy out. He seemed to know what I was thinking and intentionally did the opposite; a military general flanking his troops into a position where his enemy least expected them to strike from. I was taken aback, as I usually was by him.

"Really. Just like that. You want to live with me."

"Yes. Just like that. The timing couldn't be more perfect. Where do I sign?"

After pooling our money and visiting a few rentals we found in the paper, eventually we moved into the lower level of a moderately sized two-family home that had been converted into a three-bedroom apartment on Bollingen Road in what was considered *downtown* Ithaca. Though my parents never actually articulated their displeasure with my often inconsiderate behavior in terms of what time I came and went and what I did while I was gone, it was refreshing to know that there were no longer any sad, watchful, pitying eyes. I grew to be concerned about my mother who felt she had to stay so silent while full of so much awareness of my drinking habit. Her mother and father had been alcoholics, which, rather than embolden her outrage, guided her into a passive acceptance and meditation practice that not only permitted but also encouraged her to drift along ever lightly. She had discovered me on the porch while leaving for work on more than one occasion, passed out and covered in any number and combination of fluids and I was convinced she knew I had taken acid before she brought my sister and I to watch a presentation of *Hamlet* at Shakespeare In The Park one Thursday night in May because I spent a half hour closely studying a dry old goose turd I found in the grass before she caught me and slapped it out of my hand like I was a two-year-old holding a dry goose turd he had found in the grass.

I felt that by removing myself from their home, and thereby their line of vision, my mother and father could be content in knowing that their job of raising me was completed successfully and that they could focus all of their attention on my sister, who was still eluding all diagnosis as to her severe disability which rendered her unable to speak, walk, or fend for herself in any way despite the fact that she was thirteen years old.

My mother cried as we had our last dinner together at their kitchen table and my dad playfully mocked her for being so dramatically sensitive given the fact that I would most likely be back three or four times a week to eat their food as it was only a twenty-minute drive to my new place. My sister, Lilly, however, just smiled and gazed around the room—not lost to herself, but possessive of something unrevealed to us.

The house we would be moving into was tucked away on a side street off of the only commercial area in the city. It was built in the early nineteen-hundreds, as most houses in that part of town were, and it stood directly across the street from a Protestant church. To the right and down a few blocks was a quaint but acceptable state college district, which contained thirty coffee shops, fourteen ski and snowboard retailers, a 7-Eleven, and over 100,000 bars within a three-square-mile radius. The house was originally painted a deep blue, though large strips of it were peeling off and the vibrancy intended by the last owner was reduced to a drab groan. The front yard was small and covered in shade for the duration of the day thanks to the enormous and diseased oak trees that lined the street. Immediately inside was a foyer with a large wooden door on the left leading to the upstairs apartment and the same large wooden door on the right, behind which was our living room. That living room had enormous, filthy bay windows, a thirteen-foot ceiling, and a nonfunctioning fireplace with a mantle. Through *that* was a dining room, and off to that dining room's left was a newly refurbished kitchen with all appliances included. Walking back out the kitchen into the dining room and to your left down a long hall was one bathroom, three bedrooms, and an "office" that we could turn into a guest room, if necessary. All the rooms were painted white. We were not allowed to change that. Upstairs, the layout was exactly the same, and we knew this because when the man who would eventually be our landlord took our down payment and first month's rent, he let us stay behind and "get a feel for the place," as long as we locked up. A door in our kitchen led to a small, cold linoleum limbo between the two rentals. To our immediate left was a stairway that went half a flight down to an outside door that opened to the driveway, then made a sharp right-hand turn and descended further down into the basement. We were told we could use the basement to store boxes, but it was dark and musty and terrible. I decided to go no further, but Frank entered the darkness like one might fall into a warm bed. Backing out, I returned to the landing that our kitchen door was on, then made a sharp left up another flight of stairs to a door that was surprisingly unlocked. I entered and found an exact replica of our downstairs apartment, but with no kitchen appliances. I crept silently through the rooms as if I might be caught at any second. After looking through the closets and cabinets for anything left behind, I went out onto the patio that extended off their living room, directly above our porch, and was taken aback by a newly dead sparrow that lay at the doorframe. There weren't even any flies on it yet. Its eyes and beak were open and its wings were spread out. There wasn't any blood and nothing looked broken, almost as if it were a painting that had gently fallen from where it once hung above the door and drifted to the ground like a leaf. I remembered my grandmother once telling me that dead birds were bad luck so I kicked it off the porch into the yard like trash and went back downstairs to retrieve Frank. It was getting late and my parents would be curious as to whether or not I had actually signed a lease and depleted their bank account by the four hundred and fifty dollars they had given me via check in case we decided to take it.

Since Frank and I were still full-time students with part-time incomes, we determined that we should find one more housemate to fill the empty room in order to free up some spending money. Frank quickly suggested a friend he made in his Geometry In Art class named Evan Selene. I felt uneasy at first about allowing a someone I didn't know into our new home and pushed vehemently to get Frank to agree to let Eddie move in with us, but it turned out that Eddie was very satisfied living with his parents, paying nothing and answering to no one. He was an immovable sword lodged in the suburban stone of our mutual past. He was also the only person around with a pickup truck, so I obligated him to help me move in.

On June 2nd, 1999, I unlocked the door to my first apartment with my new set of keys and began loading in the few boxes I had filled with whatever belongings I had accrued at that point. Most were cutlery and technologies that my parents wanted to get rid of as an excuse to upgrade. Though we had walked through the place just a few weeks before, there was a slow burn in the air as I walked down the hall to my bedroom. It was like I was trespassing in someone else's empty home on someone else's valued land. I grew apprehensive as I put my few books on the shelf near where my bed would eventually go and decided I would wait out in the living room for Eddie to show up with the couch. I felt safe again when I saw him pull along the curb in front, and I hurriedly went out to greet him. He stepped out of his black Chevy pickup and placed his hands on his hips while looking intently at the front of the house, making clicking noises with his tongue at the back of his teeth.

"Nope. Not gonna work," he said in the low, thick, horrible voice of an old contractor. "Place has got too much structural damage. Gonna need all new Cannuter Brackets in each of the main load-bearing joists." He pointed to the roof and then to the tree in the front yard.

We untied the couch that my parents had given me from their basement and moved it into the living room in front of the fireplace and I offered Eddie a beer as thanks.

"I have to take my dad to his doctor's appointment in an hour—so, yeah, just four or five." I went into my book bag and took out a warm can of beer that he grabbed eagerly and drank without interruption. Then he took one last cursory glance around before nodding firmly. "Okay. See you later."

"Really? You don't want to hang out? Frank is coming with the new guy."

"No. I fucking hate Frank," he said with an erudite arrogance.

"Shut up. You do not."

"Yeah. I do. He's pure shit. He is not to be trusted."

"What? Of course he is." I looked at him like a hostage who, in the presence of their kidnappers, tells a cop that they're doing just fine.

"Fuck that. He's heartless..." Eddie moved to the doorway and began swinging his car keys around on his index finger. "I mean, I can be civil to him if I have to be. But if he looks down his crooked nose at me one more time I'm going to stomp a hole in his chest, and that's a goddam fact." I had no doubt that Eddie could, if provoked, cripple or kill a human being. He had always been ragged on for being *fat*, but he was actually built like a dad and had a dad's strength—a very unique kind of power that has no other source in the known universe. Having said what he felt to be memorable last words, Eddie got in his truck and lovingly flipped me off as he drove away honking the horn to the tune of "Firestorm" by Earth Crisis.

About a half hour later, as I experimented with couch positions, the door unlatched and Frank came in, followed by a short dark-skinned kid who appeared to be in his teens carrying a box and wearing a green zip-up hooded sweatshirt, ripped jeans, and flip flops. His hair was black and short and his stubbly beard looked like it was made of metal shavings and had been applied with a magnetic pen.

"That couch is fucking gross. Ray, this is Evan. Evan, that's Ray." Before I could appropriately respond to Frank's nasty indictment of the couch, Evan set the nondescript box down loudly at our feet and stood up to enthusiastically thrust his hand straight out at me like a spear which stopped just short of my heart. My anger subsided and I gave pause. His eyes abruptly and permanently soothed the inner tantrum Frank had riled up. And yet, concurrently, they were, without exaggeration, the wildest fucking things I had ever seen—excited bright green galaxies of an uncertain but fearless lust marching ever forward while simultaneously rooted in all, like god-kings astride proud elephants. Every layer of myself that wasn't huddled tightly around the core, was drawn calmly toward him like a well-practiced exodus from a burning office building with no force or resistance, just a stately current shifting from what was, to a valley of what was not. He had a smirk on his face like all of this—everything that was occurring and everything that had ever occurred before—was pretend. It was a smile that indicated a bond between us hired actors, ones who were made aware of this introduction previously but instructed by a higher force to keep up the pretense of an authentic introduction in front of those who willingly suspended their disbelief. It nonverbally communicated to me that the game was still afoot, and we were playing whatever roles we had assumed with an unmatched grace. I took his hand, and I remember thinking that his handshake too was pathetic. It didn't force any motion on my end. It just sat in my palm and existed, requiring me to activate the gesture. I shook it firmly.

"Hey, man. Nice to meet you."

"Good, man. I'm good," he replied, absentmindedly. Evan's enormous eyes darted around the room without blinking, as if he would never see it again and needed to commit every corner and shadow to memory in order to pass down to a future generation so the room and the light and what it all meant would never be forgotten. "Real good. Yeah. Okay. Well, this place feels totally fucking haunted."

"I was thinking the same thing!" I said, excitedly. "What is it!?" Evan got real serious and his unbreakable concentration followed an unseen vortex of energy that moved around him like an undulating swarm of birds at dusk. I still had not seen the guy blink. He shook his head steadily.

"I don't know but it's definitely here. Definitely." Evan's tone was confident.

"You feel it, Frank?" he asked.

"Nope." Frank kept his attention on the box of old sketches and charcoal and pens he had on the ground in front of him. "But I didn't smoke an infinite amount of weed on the drive over here like you did."

"Yeah, that's true." Then he turned back and looked, not at me or through me, but into me. "You smoke?" My desire to be accepted lurched forward aggressively like a manual car started up by someone only practiced in automatic, though it was put in check by a much more rational mind, one that had an allegiance to a promise I made while in the midst of a blind delirium. "Weed? No." I shook my head like the question was a fly on my skin. "Cigarettes, yes, but not weed. Not anymore."

Since my last time experimenting with marijuana (which was my third time ever, first if you consider that the two times previous were more of just a sampling of which I barely even inhaled) I had absolutely zero desire to reenter the vault. Not only because of the unguided journey through the hellish, radioactive wasteland of my psyche that ended four hours later at the base of unconquerable mountain of self hatred, but because of the caliber of people I associated with it. All the kids from my high school that smoked weed into their college days were filthy tweakers who wore the same oversized T-shirts of the same bands that they co-opted from their parents generation and the same shade of baggy acid-washed jeans. They weren't cool or progressive like Frank and Eddie. They were losers who listened to unlistenable music, smelled like burning mold and had absolutely nothing remotely funny or interesting to say, though it never stopped them from pushing their long, greasy hair behind their ears and laughing with their whole body like marionettes as they said it. They worried about nothing, nodded obliviously, smiled dumbly, and walked aimlessly. They were mentally shut into themselves. I was unable to see the appeal of or attraction to ones own inner space, particularly after the horrors that assailed me on my pathetically brief visit to my own. Nothing good happened there. It was always after midnight in the house of mirrors.

"Good. Keep it that way," Frank called out with his back still turned. "You were a complete disaster last time. I mean, it was funny to *me*, but for your sake..."

Holy hell, please don't mention that fucking picture I drew about reality being the inside of a magicians top hat, I thought as I recalled the colorful scene I had committed to a blank sheet of printer paper. To make it even more pathetic, it had been done in crayon because I rationalized that since children used crayons, I could channel an infant's relationship to God. Also I cried on it: "...as a way to sanctify."

I had actually said that part out loud to Frank at the time of my drawing it and he howled with delight at my unfortunate imprisonment in my own head. I remembered trying to convince him that what I was saying was the truth, but words were failing me utterly. The drug had rendered language useless, and as a writer, language was all I had, so the feeling of losing my medium was both stifling and liberating and that duality confounded me— left me reeling as two universes battled for a position that only one was allowed to occupy. Letters were disembodied symbols that escaped me without any attachment to the idea that I had hired them to represent. The original thought was coming down from somewhere more divine, and when they reached out for a phrase to grab and ride into the material world on, they found none. I was as good as mute, unworthy of the realizations I was having because my faculties were too underdeveloped to carry their weight. I comprehended all of this in an instant, in one sweeping and thorough moment of clarity, but before I could begin to compartmentalize which cause belonged to which effect, a bell rang and every dancer and drunken reveler fell back in line. I was again unremarkable. Just *way too high* in Frank's garage. Another typical pothead who thought he had seen something profound when shown a centuries-old trick, one that had already been demystified by the millions that had seen it before me. I cringed as I relived the dejection.

"Jesus," Evan said. "You are so judgmental." He was smiling, but this time it was out of disbelief. Evan's smile seemed to be capable of representing a thousand different things and his sharp retort shook me back into the moment. I looked at Frank who was visibly confused. Evan just stared at him in disappointment, as if sensing my nervousness.

"Maybe Ray liked it? Maybe he would do it more if you weren't making him feel like total shit about it?"

"Actually, I fucking hated it," I said. Evan's quick gaze directly into my eyes reprimanded me for interrupting the principle of the protest.

"Well, that's circumstantial," Evan said. "But I bet if you were with the right people it would be different for you." Frank shrugged, no longer phased. What I liked was none of his concern and we were wasting his time by even asking him to bother with it.

"You're way better at drinking. Stick with that." He turned back around to sort through his pens. Evan picked up his box and went down the hallway toward his room. I, however, stood teetering nervously in the middle of an infinitely long lever, waiting. All potential and no direction.

CHAPTER FIFTEEN

THE NEXT MORNING WE TOOK THE 15 OUT of Los Angeles. A decade before, after my first tour of the West Coast, Southern California served as the crest of an exalted hill. Its position on a map meant that I had geographically traveled as far as one could, which was commendable, but far too common in the music business. The only people that were truly impressed anymore were high school acquaintances on Facebook and my parents. To a musician, driving thousands of miles to play a gig was the same as driving twenty miles to your office. It was just a job. Symbolically, however, reaching the Pacific Ocean while playing my music indicated that I had journeyed to an ideological boundary in order to press my hand firmly against it, challenging its very nature in a delirious feat of audacity. But that was a long time ago, back when I was a self-righteous kid who read way too much Kerouac and thought life was beautiful and that love prevailed. Now, however, as an adult, I actually preferred to turn my back to California. So that next morning, as hungover and ashamed as I always was after nights like the ones we just raged through, Chet, Cube, and I reentered the unquestionable at sixty-five uninspired miles per hour as we had done time and time again believing nothing of the sort.

The fanciful became finite in the dun periphery of the American Southwest's mute vegetation where there are no ebbs and flows to life or land—no miracles that weren't typical, no surprises that were not accounted for. Where once there was enthusiasm in our step, all we could muster now was a whimper of relief as we trickled down slowly from state to state, through a desert that stored life's spare parts. With nothing else to do, I lay back on the couch in the front lounge of the bus, put on my headphones, and began the *Mind Magic* series I had on my phone. As the voice encouraged me to descend a flight of golden stairs toward a room where a box was hidden, my muscles relaxed and my eyes rolled back as the astral choir chimed in. This initial phase of the episode always felt exquisite, like the last full moments of a rich life. *Maybe if I could temper its acuteness*, I thought. *Maybe if I could just hover here at the crossover, suspend myself in the middle of this breakthrough, I would be all right.* I didn't need to go any closer, I was content right here. But I thought that every single time, and every single time I got greedy. Now would be no different. *Let it be louder*, I thought, as I slipped deeper in. The hum was everywhere, swaddling me. I felt ecstasy, and my eyes rolled even further back, as if evolving into a next stage of awareness. My breaths became deeper and slower and more meaningful. I was conscious of all of this, and it was beautiful. It was perfect, but it was the kind of perfection that could only exist if paired with fear.

Then there was fear. It got the nod and, once acknowledged, it exploded as viciously as havoc from the big bang. I had slipped so far in that I had actually come out the other side into a dark prenatal void. I tried to speak but there was nothing to speak with, nor knowledge of the language of memory. As I always did, I realized I needed to pull at the muscles of my neck to shake my head and startle myself awake, but at the moment I was too weak. I would need to wait until my spirit could affect form—but, of course, without lungs, the process of waiting was done breathlessly. My mouth opened and closed rhythmically, fishlike, gasping at air as if I could trap it and put it to work. Nothing.

But what if I just let it all go? I thought. *What if I let myself drift right through it? Would it pull me deeper? Would it guide me to the valley of death? If so, this is a test of my fortitude at the foot of the reaper. I have a chance to prepare, I can't squander this. I have snuck into the shadows and am not yet overtaken. Look around. Let go.* This exact conversation happened on each occurrence, and each time I panicked and gripped safety. *No,* I thought. *I need to get awake. I will be brave another day. My life is out there with my body, not here. Wake yourself up.*

I began, as I always did, by envisioning my head shaking. I saw every detail, every hair moving, every muscle expanding and contracting as if I were studying it for an exam. I needed the picture to be clear and full if I expected it to become real. I looked around the bus. Everything was under a tight white fog but I could make out their edges. Over there was the hard, white microwave. Over here was the big, black television. Sitting to my left was Cube wearing an orange hooded sweatshirt at the table looking into a computer screen. All I needed was that first whimper and I could begin making my way into the world. I tried to call out, and though it was not loud enough for anyone to hear, a sound was born from the source that traveled in vibrations along a fragile silk thread. With that allowance, I could really begin going to work. Now I saw my head thrashing madly, and on the earth, Ray twitched. Nothing massive, but a connection was made between the two planes of existence...and Ray was aware of me. I moved harder and faster, calling out increasingly louder, this time from only a few feet away.

Cube had heard me whimper and looked over.

It was a miracle. Seeing that I was in the throes of some sort of fit, he frantically stood up and lunged for me, shaking my shoulders. I breathed air and came back.

"Jesus Christ. Thank you," I said as I came to the surface.

"Dude," Cube said, shaking his head in disbelief. He was visibly nervous. I had made him aware of this condition but he had only been present for it once before, and for the first few seconds thought I was being silly while I listened to music in my headphones. "Where the fuck do you go?"

"Absolutely nowhere. It's pretty awful."

"Is it epilepsy?"

"No, I told you. It's apnea. It only happens in my sleep."

"What do you see?"

"I see everything. But it's gray. Probably because my eyes are closed and I'm just looking at what I saw right before I closed them."

"Your eyes aren't closed," he said as he took an overly dramatic step back. "They were fucking wide open and they were completely blank. I've never seen anything like it. It looked like you were dead. Except you were groaning."

"Really? They were open? I always thought they were closed." I guess I had never really had a fit in front of too many people. Hannah had been present for one or two of them, but she had slept right through. I tried to explain it to her when she was startled awake by me being startled awake but she never seemed to get it. She dismissed them as nightmares, which they were, but real ones. Well, not real, but real to me, which was the same.

"Yes. Dude. It was fucking scary. I really thought you were gone. I was seriously thinking I'd have to be the one to call your parents. You need a tour manager who doubles as a doctor. I don't get paid enough for this shit."

"It was only a few seconds."

"Didn't feel like it, man. In my head it lasted forever. I was picking out my clothes for your funeral."

"You thought I was dead so you began thinking about men's fashion?"

"Fuck you. Don't do that shit again." He put his hand on the counter and bent over slightly, breathing out deeply, recovering from the real shock of my surreal death.

A few hours later we arrived in Las Vegas.

CHAPTER SIXTEEN

THERE WAS A BAR DOWN THE STREET FROM our apartment called Merlin's that could not have been more inappropriately named in that the only magical thing about it was that it stayed in business. In order to save on utilities, there were no light bulbs. The neon beer taps provided all the light necessary for patrons to sign their tabs, and from outside, the illumination of the moon and its minions of streetlights could be counted on to creep nervously through the dirty front windows and settle uncomfortably on the warped floorboards like people arriving at their first séance. In the winter months, the ambiance was also enhanced by the light from a fireplace that could be tended to by anyone who brought their own wood which, oddly, most people did.

There was a dartboard that was impetuously placed against the half back wall perpendicular to the bar where, if used, stood to put oblivious seated patrons at severe risk, particularly the owner—a man named Big Lou who had a piss-colored beard and was always passed out atop his stool with his disgusting head on the pine. There was a stage in the very far back up a few stairs to the left of the dartboard with what looked to be a decent sound system, though for the first month not a single soul took advantage of the open mic they reserved it for, maybe because Big Lou never cared to advertise it or maybe because the clientele was exclusively sad, old alcoholics who knew that drinking was more about loss and suffering on earth than about singing and dancing above it. The doorman, whom we heard referred to as Cube, was lenient about admitting people who were pitiful enough to voluntarily hang out there, so even though I always came equipped with a fake ID that said I was a twenty-eight-year-old named Michael Korsakoff, he very rarely checked it. Frank and Evan and I crossed his bridge almost every night of the week for that first year with him rarely saying a word.

Despite all of this, Merlin's eventually began to feel like ours, or rather, *we* began to feel like *its*. I was being matriculated into the city—that enormous, shape-shifting, dream-like pantheon of rust and snow that had once, many years prior, allowed me access to my own soul by way of the abnormal, beautiful songs it played through Mr. Reilley's car speakers. I felt so thankful sitting at a bar just being ignored by the old townies, and when I drank there by the fire I was full of such confusing joy that I couldn't even articulate it. I felt comfortable with my friends in a room where death went to practice its art. Every moment was saturated with brilliant newness and as the frenzied moments passed, I could only reach out and hope to feel its wind before the next was upon me. I stood in the middle of the thruway amidst the speeding traffic of time. The future and the past were boring ideas in comparison.

My housemates and I had become entwined. What developed between us as weeks passed was not just preferred, but imperative, unlike my dwindling interactions with Eddie or Aaron. When judged next to the members of my new life, Eddie looked more like a disseminator of cheap gossip and incomplete contrarian theories than an actual friend. And if he could be coaxed from his parents home, the topics of our brief conversations felt antiquated and the mood overwhelmingly didactic, though this may have been less a sudden epiphany as it was a long overdue that I come to terms with what I had secretly felt all along—that I wasn't special to him, no matter how badly I wished. Our past was a static brotherhood rooted in nothing but rituals and tradition, but the present I had with Frank and Evan was undulating and parental. Frank, like a strict father whose praise and approval I longed for, was lustrous and dangerously knowing, while Evan was so gentle and possessive of such a motherly nobility and humble virtuousness that I could not imagine being apart from him.

Like parents, they often conflicted in front of me, and when they did I could do nothing but retreat into my room and play the guitar that I had recently been lured into playing again at Evan's behest. My father had introduced me to the guitar when I was around two years old. It was a 1973 Gibson Hummingbird and it was the first flower I had ever laid eyes on. For my eleventh birthday I asked if I could have one of my own, and when I came downstairs for breakfast before going to school that morning, there against the wall next to the table stood—as tall as I was—a guitar case–shaped gift with a bow on it. I knew exactly what it was. My fathers guitar. I lost the plot.

"I don't want YOUR guitar," I screamed. "I want my own." My parents were visibly confused and hurt, and I was glad for it. My dad unwrapped it for me and put it around my neck and it felt like it covered my entire being. I was infinitesimally small standing behind it. He strummed it a few times thinking that the sound would placate me, but it didn't. My heart was broken. I knew I couldn't make the music my dad made with such little hands and arms that didn't even reach around the body. I didn't have the strength or the size to meet the demands of whatever it was inside me that had ordered me to play.

"It's too big!" I yelled at him, sobbing. Hurt and disappointed, my father gently pulled it off me and put it back in its case, locking the clasps like a warden locks a cell.

"Then you can play it when you're big enough." I never saw him touch that guitar again. A fire only spreads away from its source, it never returns.

Depending on how one chose to look at it, it was either a curse or a blessing that I was getting quite good quite fast, as it was purely a result of frequent and lengthy practice sessions held privately while two heads of the hydra gnashed their teeth at each other. Usually they fought when Frank was drunk, though Evan didn't argue as much as he passively dismissed Frank's anger, which made Frank angry enough to storm out and vanish for days on end. Evan would capitalize on the silence in our house by meditating—a practice I had been made familiar with from my mother years ago, but had never had any interest in learning for many of the same reasons that I was hesitant to be associated with potheads. As he sat cross-legged under headphones on a pillow in the middle of the floor of his dark, bare walled room, I would sit on the bed in mine and do finger stretch exercises or listen closely to the white noise for a few uniquely related chords. This would continue for hours, not a word spoken between us as we filled the house with our own emanations of personal bliss that fused to each other under the roof like particles.

Whenever it was that Frank could finally pull himself from the low clouds and return home, he had a tendency to sit down immediately at his massive black drawing desk in the living room where he would stay the night, turning whatever it was that he had seen while he was away into startling illustrations. With livid fluidity he would draw deep into the page as if carving soft wood, scooping it up with the tip of his pencils and shoving it aside like an earthmover altered the land and could, on a divine whim, reappear suddenly from his valleys at the surface of the desk in order to mold the shavings like clay into proud busts before dashing to the crest of his new mountains and summoning a great storm, taking what wasn't and turning it into what was and visa versa. It was like watching a magician shuffle cards—the things you saw were impressive but not nearly as mystic as the things you didn't. The lead would swirl lovingly at terrifying depths, aware of death but unconcerned. Frank was a vulgar lover of his muse, abusing her before caressing her, and one could only look on in embarrassing silence feeling sickened by your own awe as the two of them fused and disbanded in violent rhythm with complete disregard for the morality of the crowd that gathered.

Evan and I would sometimes stand quietly behind him whenever we recognized that he was deep in his work, though I couldn't be certain that Frank ever noticed us there over his shoulder, so true was his aim. He didn't exclusively draw when vexed, but those sessions seemed to be the most intense. Sometimes he would sit for a few hours after classes, drinking beer, writing brief descriptions of what would go where, piecing the bones together before attempting to drape it in skin. I watched him so often and admired him so greatly that I became familiar with his process, and eventually came to understand that Frank was more of a mathematician huddled over an equation that represented some unflinching law of our existence than he was a painter squinting into a kaleidoscope of color and form begging to be translated into personal experience. While astoundingly complex, his drawings were beautiful because they were base and true and they spoke directly to a part of me that I knew was there but had forgotten how to worship, some ancient emotional relic. They were fundamental, stripped to the blueprints of our common mythology. Gorgeously written origin stories spread without a sound. They came from somewhere that could be seen by all if looked at closely and proven to exist if thought about hard enough, but they were only calculated to look whimsical. Not inspired as much as formulated. Frank was a genius, yes, but he was no artist, though he did inspire me to wonder if that isn't what true art actually is—a cold, technological understanding of how to manufacture your own inspiration. As I watched him one night, lost to everyone but himself, I knew that not since I was a kid had *I* heard a voice so clear that it drove me to create something truly new. My first step was inspired, and so was my first word and my first kiss with Hannah. *But now?* I was nearing my twenties and that kind of thing was foolish and must be abandoned like all other childish things. I would need to learn how to create my own *inspiration* because I was tired of waiting for someone to speak through me. It wouldn't be as refined as it once may have been, but it would look like the real thing no matter how diluted the effects became by age. If one is fooled by magic, then isn't the magic as good as real? I knew that Frank would be my teacher. The balance I had so strenuously been keeping in that house had now tipped, and once again, as I had on the night we met, I found myself coming back to life in his presence. The earth breathed and an enormous tension was released.

CHAPTER SEVENTEEN

THE TWO DAYS FOLLOWING A SOLD-OUT Vegas show were off days, one of which we would be spending in Phoenix on our way to Dallas, Texas. Hannah called early that morning as we crossed the border from Nevada into Arizona, but I declined it, and let it go to voicemail, which I would never listen to because voicemails were lectures that made me feel helpless and agitated. Plus, I had to muster the nerve to call Evan and let him know what time we would be arriving. She would understand.

"Well, well, well," Evan said, picking up the phone on the first ring.

"Evan. This is Raymond."

"Raymond? Or Ray?"

"We'll be pulling into town around six."

"Fantastic. Just text me when you're close. I'll come and scoop Raymond. Leave Ray on the bus." He hung up. Cube stumbled out of his bunk into the lounge at around 10:00 a.m.

"We have today and tomorrow off. Why aren't you drinking yet?" I asked him.

"Holy shit, it's already time to clock in?" Cube referred to having his first drink of the day as "clocking in," and preferred to have someone join him, though he was not above drinking all alone. He went over to the cabinets next to the fridge and grabbed down a bottle of Jameson, opened it, and emptied a fourth of it down his enormous red throat. He gasped and blinked hard.

"So smooth," Cube said sarcastically as he faked vomiting and let a strand of drool run off his bottom lip. "Must be barrel aged."

"Don't forget the steroids. Gotta mix up a nice cocktail of hormones and whiskey to really get life movin' in the right direction."

"Thank you for reminding me, Ray. Get up. Let's do this." He flipped open his bag that was on the bench and dug around in it for a few seconds before retracting his hand. Inside was a small glass bottle and a syringe in a paper and clear plastic envelope.

"No. I fucking hate this," I said, crossing my arms. "I don't back you using them, and your butt sucks. Shove them in your own ass."

"Don't be such a pussy."

"Not wanting to put a needle full of speed into a grown friend's ass does not make me a pussy. It's probably very normal for people who are not doctors to feel that way." I said.

"Fine. We're not friends. My good pal Chet will do it. *Chet!*" He announced into the bunk area, "Please put your dick away and come help me take steroids." From behind a curtain on the floor on the left side of the alley one heard a shuffling of papers and then saw the animal emerge.

"What the fuck are you doing in there?" Cube asked.

"I was trying to jerk off," Chet said, candidly.

"Why were there papers rustling?"

Chet looked at him like he didn't understand the question for a few seconds before he arrived at the answer.

"Because magazines are made of paper you dipshit." At this, Cube exploded with laughter, but Chet just stared blankly.

"You jerk off to magazines?" I asked, incredulous. "You have an iPad and a phone and a computer that connects to the internet where all the good porn is, and you jerk off to a magazine?"

"It's not all on the internet. Some of it is in my magazine."

Cube spoke very slowly and blinked hard as he did. "Why. Do you. Use. Magazines?"

"Makes me feel like a kid again."

"So you prefer to jerk off your child self. Gotcha. What magazine do you use?" Cube asked. Chet went back to his bunk and shamelessly pulled out some adult editorials.

"Well, these are all *Juggs* but I have a subscription to *Swank*."

"In this, the two thousand and twelfth year of our Lord, you have a subscription to a pornographic magazine?"

"You don't even have a fucking house, you derelict." Cube shouted, almost angrily. "You live on the road. Where do they get sent to?"

Chet sat on the couch, arms outstretched along the back, his disgusting hairy torso displayed through his sleeveless and unbuttoned Hawaiian shirt. "My girlfriends house."

"You have a girlfriend. And you send pornographic magazines to her house." I was at the stage where I could only repeat the information as a way to make my head try to make sense of it.

"Yes, for like the past three months. Thanks for paying attention to my life."

"Oh, I'm sorry. You just fucked that horrible girl in Seattle. Forgive me for thinking you were single."

"What does fucking someone have to do with being in love with someone else?"

I said nothing.

"Will someone please help me take these illegal enhancements already? I'm getting weaker by the second."

Chet reluctantly took the needle and plunged it deep into Cube's exposed ass cheek with one powerful thrust, and as I thought about what Chet had just asked me I grew despondent. I hadn't spoken to Hannah in over a day. I didn't say goodnight to her or tell her I was safe and alive. I took out my phone and texted her that I loved her because it was true and I needed it to stay true forever or I would finally be brave enough to let go and surely I would die. I looked at the screen and read the text I had written over and over and over, studying the letters closely like I was looking through a fog at the edges of the muscles that pulled the heart until they too became real.

CHAPTER EIGHTEEN

I SHADOWED FRANK, MAKING HIM ALMOST AS much of a priority as my guitar. In fact, I was only playing my guitar anymore as a way to prove to him that I too could be methodical, that the chords were placed in an order according to a concise musical theory and the lyrics were plugged into their allotted spaces like words into a crossword puzzle designed by the precision of rhythm and time. Not only unimpressed by me, he seemed unmindful of me, as any master might this early in our schooling. But I was an eager apprentice, and the ease with which he locked away his affection only pushed me to play better and inspired me to plot and doubt and analyze and argue with a desperate passion, one which began to draw a very palpable division in the apartment between Evan and I. We connected less often, though this was not due to a lack of things to say (on the contrary, there was a distinct, deeply felt, but unspoken love for his calm) as much as it was the feeling that he looked upon me with nonjudgmental disappointment similar to the one conveyed by my mother on the mornings she found me on the porch, and it broke my heart. I felt unclean when around Evan. He no longer held on to a fantasy about my potential as a writer, so I decided it would be better to deny myself the gift of being in his presence. In a sense, it was a way to expiate my new indulgences. He never seemed sore with me, just detached from my antics during the nights spent out drinking and womanizing with Frank. Often I wished that he would pull me aside and yell at me or get drunk and hit me like a normal human being who was simply fed up, but it never happened. So while he smiled at me, I knew he didn't belong to me anymore. He belonged entirely to himself or something greater. Not less. Not me.

"Evan is such a tweaker," I said to Frank one night at Merlin's, initiating gossip he hadn't asked for but might happily encourage.

"Fuck is a tweaker?"

"You know. He's just completely oblivious. Like he doesn't notice the obvious rift in the house." As I had decided earlier that afternoon, drawing attention to a rift might plant the idea in Frank's head that he and I were a team against a common enemy, siblings on a foreign field.

"Maybe he does and doesn't care." Frank took a swig of beer.

"So he doesn't care that you and I are getting closer together?"

"Who knows what he's thinking, man. He's not your fucking wife." Frank hadn't taken the bait. He hadn't seemed flattered, nor did he reassure me that I was correct in my perception. I felt a dizzying loss and pulled back to regain footing. I quietly took a sip of my beer. When Frank spoke again, I was relieved.

"I don't think he thinks much at all, to be honest. He's on that meditation shit, and even when he's awake, it's like he's dreaming all the fucking time. He's just not on my level. That smirk bugs the shit out of me. He's going insane. It's aggravating, because you can't talk reasonably with him. There are fucking bills to pay down here on earth, dude," Frank said with a smile. "And letting God take the wheel isn't going to get them paid."

Because I understood exactly what Frank meant, I felt myself naturally pulling in closer, cutting away even more of the fat that hung from the marmoreal form that would one day be my self. We were kindred, and the more he said that fit into the overlooked compartments of my brain, the more real I appeared to everyone else looking upon us. It was absurd to believe in God, I had come to understand that now. There was no proof of him anywhere anymore. In fact, the very existence of war, famine, heartache, loss, grief, and Lilly was all evidence against it. There was no *plan* for us. We are a misspelling being erased by Death in order for the story of total chaos to continue, an accidental growth like the one inside of Eddie's father, that begins independently of need under certain conditions which, given the infiniteness of space, would have to happen somewhere and all of our advances are just the inevitable progression of bacteria outthinking its hosts and auditioning new survival techniques. The cosmos do not care that we're looking into its window with handmade eyes from our cold little outpost in the black woods, it will continue devouring unabated and if at any point I fear being consumed, it's just my fear of missing out being amplified. There's no soul that will outlive us. We are merely a blip, a puff of air, a flit of disarray that will one day go right back onto the pile to be shoveled into the furnaces that drive the universe blindly and loudly forward because death is the only thing life needs from us and if it needed anything more, it would tell us—yet it never has. Not a peep from it. Our existence was accidental and we can do nothing about that now except enjoy our senses as they explode before vanishing. *We* may have shown up when things got really interesting, but I didnt expect there to be any more favors.

I had subconsciously been feeling this sense of nihilism for a long time, maybe having stumbled upon it with Eddie or maybe even earlier as a direct result of my expulsion from school, but with Frank's guiding hand, the nervous whispers of a struggle with God turned into confident declarations of rebellion against Him. No telescope could reveal divinity to be behind any of this. All that those lenses served to prove was how insignificant we are and how selfishly crazy we had been for ever thinking otherwise. There was nothing above science and reason, only below it, things that could be predicted and measured and witnessed. We were accidentally born of chaos and would eventually die of it, and chaos will go on being exactly what it is and what it was and what it will always be with no notice of us whatsoever—and that powerlessness has left us no choice but to do what we're compelled to do…while we still can…before we are dashed into an abyss by our own weak cells, where not even the things we love most can echo.

"I think you should do an open mic here," Frank said, straight down into his empty bottle. "I hear you playing all the time at home. Your songs are pretty good." It pained him to be honest with me, I could tell, but my heart took flight.

"Really?"

"Yeah. I think it would be good for you."

I had not even considered that option. In all the nights I'd gone there, I hadn't once thought to take that dark stage in the back and play my guitar in front of other people. It was there the entire time and only now, after Frank pointed it out, did I notice.

"Actually," he continued, finally looking up and around. "Go get your shit. I'll tell Big Lou you're playing tonight."

I threw my head back and laughed a mocking, disingenuous cackle like the one that I would eventually learn to recognize him by. "Not a fucking chance am I doing it now. Maybe soon, but *absolutely* not now."

At this point, Frank was smiling and looking quite determined, no doubt a little looser from the beers we had been drinking. "You can't just let them watch, Ray. You have to make them look. It's the perfect time." He turned around in his chair, away from the fire to face the bar. "LOU!" he shouted "My friend is going to play his guitar for awla you drunks." He looked at me and smiled, and his eyes were a little glazed and unfocused. Lou didn't even flinch.

"Who gives a fuck," the dirty old bar owner muttered back.

"You heard the man. Who gives a fuck. Go." Frank pointed out the window toward the enormous glowing moon.

I don't remember what happened next. I didn't plan on walking out that door and down to our place and back to the bar with my father's Hummingbird in hand, nor did I actively participate in the process, but it definitely happened and it was irreversible, like a newborn turtle rushing toward the sea. Something that I couldn't begin to understand had urged me on, and while doing so it had shanghaied my naysaying brain, binding up and blindfolding all apprehension while it moved me somewhere beyond myself. Fifteen minutes later I found myself on stage at Merlin's, a microphone in my face and a guitar in hand. I remembered where I began, and I understood where I ended up, but the space between was lost to me. There was a glaring answer to the *what*, and we could deduce the *how*, but the *why* escaped me entirely. I couldn't remember that walk for the life of me and I never would be able to.

I played the five songs I had written like it was the only purpose I had on earth, and for all I knew, maybe it really was. My fingers glided, as if possessed, over the strings and back while my voice effortlessly reached and conquered each note. I kind of just shifted to the side and stood in awe as it happened, like I wasn't there. Like it wasn't me. When I walked offstage, nobody clapped except Frank, but the next week someone else did, and by that spring there was a good handful of people who applauded. And in the summer there were even more. That fall the bar on open mic night could have been considered crowded by some and by winter, almost a year to the date from when I had first stood there, you could barely move.

The clientele had changed dramatically, much to the displeasure of Big Lou who had never intended to worry about placing large orders of beer from retailers in order to accommodate a thirsty crowd of college students or to have to "fix the bathroom" when he opened the place thirty years prior. He had obviously wanted it to be a quiet, exclusive club of the eternally damned, but, as music is wont to do, it filled the room with new life. It was now full of art students who considered dive bars *ironic*, and didn't want to suffer the awful company of alpha males who stood in the middle of dance floors throughout other parts of the city, throbbing to the music like an open artery and drenched in sweat. The drinks were cheap and strong. It was funny to watch some of the stately old drunks shocked back to life by the electric conversation of curious, if not patronizing, girls. The topics discussed between the throngs of new drinkers were deep and meaningful. And they clapped. They approved.

Even the beautiful girl with deep, black hair the color of endlessness tied up in a bun atop her brilliant head that watched me from afar. The one with eyes the color of hot sand behind thick bright red glasses and the shining, masterly lips that were incapable of sculpting anything bad out of the infinitely large marble slab of life over the brief years I would let her love me. Claire, who had the softest white skin I had ever held. Claire, who was an artist and a dancer and who listened to The Pixies and who laughed like it was a song she sang to a Queen. Claire, who captivated me with the refined majesty of her inhumanly flawless heart. She was the embodiment of a fantasy that was dreamt up the moment I first heard music and had dwelt upon ever since.

"We learned of a quote today in class that I thought was very interesting," Claire said as she sat up straight, assuming a stately poise on the porch of my apartment a month later.

"Which was?"

"Hegel said that all things of great importance in history occur twice."

"Oh yeah? Why is that interesting?"

"Because it means if we haven't done this before, we get to do it again." Then she closed her eyes and leaned in to kiss me and in one way or another I stayed right there, suspended at the precipice of her lips in soft divinity for the rest of my cruel life.

CHAPTER NINETEEN

THE BUS GOT INTO PHOENIX AT 5:30 P.M. and parked near a mall so that Cube and Chet could treat themselves to a full evening of shitty food and action movies before drinking themselves blind on overpriced drinks at an Applebee's, like they always did on days off, while our silent bus driver takes a cab to his hotel room, to sleep, and do whatever else it is that bus drivers do when they are not responsible for the lives of a few hyper-privileged entertainers. Evan came to meet me in his dusty old blue Jeep Liberty that was already waiting in the lot when we pulled in. The driver's side door was open and he was standing outside of it in the light of a retreating sun smoking a joint and wearing a green hoodie much like the one he had worn on the day we met, though this one was a little tighter around the midsection as it fought uncomfortably against his beer belly. His blue jeans were ripped and baggy, his beard was completely inconsiderate of his face, and though his eyes seemed a bit more dull and far off than I remembered, his smile was bursting with love. As I stepped off the bus I could hear Brian Wilson's sleepy voice oozing out of the faulty stereo system:

"...now how can I say it and how can I come on..."

I approached him nervously, put my bag down at my feet, and hugged him for a very long time, allowing the old nastiness that milled about in my heart to excuse itself without sound. The sacred place where Evan kept himself seemed to house no past; his life would be as it had always been—a series of photographs of an arrow in flight, each one knowing nothing of the one before or having any influence on or consideration of the ones that followed. That new moment of ours in the parking lot hadn't pondered the millions preceding it in which we were angry and proud and it made no promise of the eternity is worth of moments to come in this life or the next. It appeared only to belong to itself, and then was gone again, leaving simply the impression of a trajectory when looked at from afar. Evan finally pulled away and put his hands on my shoulders like you might see a father do to his son in an old movie about war.

"Okay," was all he said. Then he smiled, turned around, smacked the hood of his car with his open hands and got behind the wheel. I had never seen him so intense, though I was all too familiar with the telltale signs. Refusing to entertain such thoughts so early, I threw my overnight bag into the backseat. The sky was still and confidently mauve as we drove a few quiet miles through a dim Arizona wind. There was simply no reason to speak and neither of us cared to look for one. I felt no pressure to entertain him with tales of the road and he seemed to be mindful and accepting of the evening, looking wildly at the mountains as he chain-smoked, unconvinced of my presence.

After a quiet twenty minutes we pulled into the driveway of a ranch-style home that was so small and thoughtlessly designed I couldn't believe his quirky parents had agreed to purchase it for him, though an unassuming, lifeless residence might be a perfect place to hide a recovering addict. Behind the house, however, the mountains stood almost as tall as the evening sun, impinging upon it as they pushed up through the bottom of the sky. I couldn't feel anything but awe as I approached the property from the east. This house could have sprawled over a hundred acres and erupted proudly ten stories into the blue, but when seen against such effortless fortunes of nature, the differences between mansion and shack became too trivial to heed and his basic abode became as grand as any house.

"This view is incredible," I said as we approached the door. Evan unlocked it and squatted, bracing himself for something he knew to be approaching.

"Yeah. Wait until you see it from the backyard." As he said this, a colossal grey and white animal galloped toward him at full speed from the back of the house, clomping rhythmically against the ceramic tiles that lined the entire floor. In the odd but universally recognized *I'm talking to a good dog* voice, Evan greeted the enormous monster by taking his beach ball–sized head in between his hands, standing it up on its hind legs and tossing it gently back and forth while repeating his name between clenched teeth.

"Samsa. Saaaaaaamsssssssaaaa." The dog was clumsy but gentle, dropping endless fistfuls of thick gray fur from its back while being shaken like someone was emptying out a pillowcase full of an old mans hair. It moaned and playfully gnashed its sharp teeth.

Evan dropped the beast onto all fours and smacked at its tail as it trotted off toward the kitchen and around a corner.

"It's an Alaskan malamute," he said very slowly and concisely, accentuating each syllable with grand mouth gestures. "I got him before I moved out here because he was made for the snow but he's a little…"—he paused and looked for the least offensive way to say what he was thinking—"*purposeless*…now without it?"

"Can't you shave him or something? Make him feel a little more comfortable in this ungodly heat?"

"I actually did that once." Evan replied, enthusiastically zipping his finger across the width of his body as if wiping a slate clean. "He got very depressed. Lost all of his confidence. Sulked for weeks. I felt terrible for him. He's just not where he knows he belongs."

He threw his keys onto a table next to the door and picked up my bag, leading me past the obviously forgotten and unloved living room on the right down an undecorated hallway to the first of two bedrooms on the opposite side.

"This one is the guest room," he said as he shoved open a wooden door.

"No, it's not. This is your dog's room."

"Okay, you are correct. This one is the dog's room."

There was an obscene amount of fur on an old white couch that was placed against the wall, as well as on the red rug in front of it that the sun fell directly onto through a window across the room. Next to the window was a small computer desk and on it, covered in a layer of dust, was what looked to be the first home computer ever invented. The black high-back chair that was turned toward us was faded and ripped, and an impressive collection of old circuit boards and tools were strewn about, indicating the presence of an obsessive tinkerer, though they too were coated with a light dusting of dog hair. The room gave me the feeling that I had stumbled across the lab of a deceased genius. Nothing hung on the walls. It was startlingly simple considering how much energy Evan had once possessed. On the floor near what I figured to be a closet door was an ashtray piled high with old marijuana cigarettes.

"Are you really going to make me sleep in here?" I said, visibly disgusted.

"Well, if it's nice enough tonight you can sleep outside on one of the lawn chairs. That's usually where I end up. Or the kitchen floor." He giggled and exited the room. After a few steps he pointed to another entrance.

"Here's the bathroom," he said without stopping. "And here's my room." He continued hurriedly past it into the kitchen, but I fell back and poked my head in to discover a sleeping space that mirrored the one he had kept when we lived together more than a decade prior—a mattress without a frame lay in the corner where two bare walls met and a lamp stood next to it on the ground. Clothes and books and records were everywhere. A familiar stereo system sat under one of the windows. "And here's the kitchen," he called out as if to distract me from a closer inspection. "Raymond. Come have a beer."

I joined him at a large table in the middle of the room. "You still have the exact same stereo," I said in slight astonishment. Evan smiled and nodded, reached into the fridge, twisted open a bottle and handed it to me, then did the same for himself.

"Why should I throw away something I can so easily fix?"

CHAPTER TWENTY

IN THE WINTER OF 2001, A BAND CALLED Alkaline Trio had booked a show in town, and according to the venue promoter—who was a friend of Frank's—they needed a local opening act in hopes of selling more tickets. Just as he had done at Merlin's, Frank volunteered me without consultation. On paper, this made him my manager and, as such, he was entitled to ten percent of whatever pay I was to receive, which would be exactly five dollars. It was a selfish act of charity, but being that it was inarguably beneficial for me I had no leverage with which to fault him for his intuitive opportunism and couldn't even hope to do so without sounding unappreciative. I was cornered by his manipulative public virtue. There was no choice left but to play my songs and share the spoils.

"They need to put your name on the flyers," he told me as we sat one night drinking whiskey and water at a bar called Father Baker's where the floors were crooked and sticky, the walls were covered in pseudo-philosophical black marker musings, the cocaine was bountiful, and the jukebox played only The Rolling Stones. I hadn't ever been on a flyer before. Up until that point, my semi-weekly open mic night performances were advertised only through word of mouth. "So you're going to have to come up with a stage name."

"Why do I need a stage name?" I asked with a half smile, trying to downplay my excitement. "Why can't I just use my real name?"

"Because it's too human. That, and people who see your last name don't even know how to fucking pronounce it. All those Polish names have like five consonants at the end without any vowel between them." He turned his stool toward me. "This is a big deal, Ray. You're an undeniable talent and you have a real chance at making a legit career out of this. But if you keep going down into the world your fans live in, they'll never see you as something special. Your real name is a mortal name. Now you need one that is immortal, the one that takes the high stage and plays above the rest. You can't be immortal and mortal at the same time."

"Okay. I get that." I thought for a second. "Can I at least keep Raymond?"

"No, but you can keep Ray. Raymond sounds like an old man and nobody wants to be *like* or be *with* an old man. Now pick a last name."

"Frank, I have no idea how to pick a new last name. There are too many things to consider."

"Then don't think about it. Look around. The answer is probably here somewhere." I began scanning the room. Ray Megatouch. Ray DivorcedFather. Ray OverweightGothGirl. Ray HealthCodeViolation. Ray GoldenElvisBust.

"Goldman," I blurted out. Frank leaned in closer. "Say that again?"

"Gold. Man." I said, annunciating slowly. "Like that Elvis," tipping my bottle toward the spray-painted bust that sat under a red light behind the register. "A gold man."

"It's good. Ray Goldman. That's a good name. I like it." He reached out and shook my hand, making it official. "Welcome."

•

RAY GOLDMAN HAD AN uncanny command of the stage the night of his first performance opening for Alkaline Trio. He and his small but loyal fan base flawlessly exchanged the room's energy, moving it back and forth like the sea and the shore trading waves, stunning undulations that lifted him up to breathtaking heights before gently setting him down again on earth. It wove around his hands and face, playfully twisting in the warmth of the light that shone down on him like an old cat. He was out of my body. When he left the stage after his set and regrouped in the tiny dressing room the venue had reserved for him, he was met by Matt, the singer of the headlining band. Matt's eyes were wide and curious, an upside-down cross hung from around his neck, and his thinning hair sat atop his head like short pale flames. He knocked as he opened the door.

"Ray," he said excitedly. "We haven't formally met. I'm Matt." He came through the door of my dressing room and hugged me like we had known each other for years. "I just wanted to thank you for opening this show. Very impressive stuff, man. Very far out stuff."

"Oh. Thanks," I said humbly. "That's nice of you. Thanks for having me." I leaned back against the wall and threw my sweaty white T-shirt over my shoulder, desperately searching for something interesting to say but Matt continued.

"It's also very feminine. It makes tough guys like me feel like it's okay to be weak. To release the woman within," he laughed. "That's rare. That's special. Do you have any records out or anything?" He asked as he took a swig of his beer. "I'd like to show some people."

"Really?"

"Yeah, man. Definitely. Definitely. I think the guys at our label would really eat this up."

"I have a few songs that I recorded in my room," I said, modestly. "Nothing professional. The bass is way too loud on it. And I was kinda sick that day, so the vocals aren't the best. Might have to pan it all the way to the left, too, if you're listening on headphones."

"Holy shit, Ray. This sounds like a terrible listening experience."

"It is."

"I don't care. They'll get the idea. These label guys are good at getting the idea."

I reached down into my backpack that rested on the couch next to a warm case of complimentary beer and pulled out one of the ten cassette tapes I had dubbed to sell at that night's show.

"What is this? No cover slip? No song titles?" Matt asked as he flipped it over and over again, surveying it for any sign of its content.

"No. I don't have names yet. Sorry."

"You're so green. The gold man is green!" he yelled, proudly, looking around for somebody—*anybody*—to appreciate his wordplay. There was no one but me, and I only laughed because I was so nervous. "It's adorable. It's really adorable." He leaned in and hugged me again. "We're going to sort you out. Wait here." He disappeared down the hall and returned a minute later with a blank piece of paper. "Nobody will listen to a tape that looks like this. We have to give it form." Setting his beer down, Matt began folding the paper around the cassette tape to the exact dimensions of the case it came in. "Gimme a pen," he said. I handed him one from my bag. "Okay…Ray…Goldman," he said aloud as he wrote it on the spine. "Now. How many songs are on here?"

"Three," I said.

"Well, you're going to need more songs, that much is obvious. But first things first. What are their names?

"I haven't named them yet."

"Ray!" Matt said, leaning his face in toward mine. "If you had three children, would you wait until you sent them to school to give them a name?"

I laughed again, still as nervously. "No, of course not."

"Then let's name them. You and me. Let's go." I looked over the page of handwritten lyrics that flashed into my head, waiting for a word or a phrase to jump out at me. The first one appeared.

"Okay, number one is called 'Morning Moon.'"

"That's nice," Matt said, writing it down. "I like that."

"Second one I guess can be called," again I mentally scanned the lyrics, "'Tigers of Detroit.'"

"Okay." He scribbled it down. "Last one?"

"That one can be called, 'Biology.'"

Matt wrote it down and flipped the paper so what would eventually be the cover was facing up. "Now we need something for the cover. Can you draw?"

"Not at all."

"Me neither. Okay, so we keep it simple." He looked up and away, searching the far corners of his brain for something to stand out. After a few seconds he came back with it. He hunched over and drew a circle. Then in the middle of the circle he put a small black dot. "There you go. It's the alchemic symbol for gold. Fitting, no? Goldman?" He handed me the new layout. It wasn't stunning, but it was far more presentable than it had been a few minutes ago

"Yeah," I said, folding and unfolding it again. "I think it works. I like it."

"Wonderful. You're ready for the world." He shoved the newly completed tape into his back pocket and handed me one of my own warm beers. "You like drugs? Come with me. Let's get lost."

CHAPTER TWENTY-ONE

"**C**OME OUTSIDE," EVAN SAID, grabbing a few more beer bottles between his fingers and a bottle of whiskey in his open hand and pulling back the sliding glass door with his elbow. He led me out onto a slab of concrete upon which sat two reclined lawn chairs with a small glass table between them. At the feet of the chairs was a small electric fountain that filled the yard with a sound of slowly moving water. About ten yards beyond that, just past a shoddy chain fence, the dry darkness started its race outward and upward toward the peaks of brown hills.

"Wow. Your parents have done really well for yourself," I said, smiling, as I allowed Samsa outside shutting the door behind him.

"Siddown. Relax." He plopped his unshapely body down in the chair and laid back, crossing his ankles. I swung a leg over the other chair, straddling it upright facing the darkness, and Samsa laid to my right, positioned stoically like a Sphinx. The air was so warm and still it made you feel like your skin didn't even exist, as if your blood was just hovering above ground like the bottom of a spring that didn't yet know its top half had started falling. I let the last few seconds of silence carry out. Then, taking a sip of beer and awkwardly peeling the corner of the label, I capitalized on what may have been my only chance to ruin everything.

"No offense, Evan, but I'm really glad I never took your advice. I don't think we'd be here right now if I had." I glanced over at him half wincing, but he continued to look forward, unmoved. I couldn't get a read. The soft jab seemed to have no discernible effect, like he didn't feel me there at all. I used the silence to recharge for another shot, but before my tank was full again, he opened his mouth, took an audible breath in and spoke slowly, never breaking his gaze toward where the horizon would have been had the mountains not so rudely interrupted.

"I'm not sure *exactly* what you're referring to?" He looked at me then looked back at the distance. "But if it got us here? And you are happy? Then I'm glad, too." He punctuated his response with a raising of his bottle as if to offer me a cheer. It was both magnanimous and astoundingly precise, somehow even seeming *correct*, like we were talking in numbers rather than heavily biased outlooks, but the ease with which he solved it only further frustrated a starved predator who watched angrily as the dinner meat was moved to a spot where his chain would not allow him to reach. The clouds that rolled out in the distance began to flicker with soft lightning. I took another pull from the beer bottle and breathed heavily, descending further.

"You know what I mean. When you told me I should stop being a writer. I'm saying that if I had stopped writing—like you advised..."—I paused to add a few careful brushstrokes to the ugly picture of him I was painting—"...I wouldn't be here right now. We wouldn't be here together. Having this beer on the back porch of the house your rich parents handed you."

I went back to my corner confidently. I had emitted too much dirt into the space between us for him too see through it or hope to make any sense of what I had done. There was no way he could have seen that coming, how could he even respond? The mask would crack. Something inside of me had come for a dogfight and it wouldn't leave without one. *Become wrath*, I thought, visualizing the antagonist in *Se7en*. Evan took another measured breath before speaking. Without warning and somewhat unfairly, he retaliated even more calmly than before.

"Raymond. I said you should stop acting like a writer. I didn't say you should stop writing." Then he laughed lightly, the type of response you have when you clearly see the answer to a problem that has plagued you, the kind of laugh that stands tall in the middle of flooding waters and weathers centuries worth of storms. *The immortal laugh of sanity.* "For someone as keen on words as you, how can you not know what so many of them actually mean?"

I was taken completely aback, knocked wildly out of cadence with a gentle touch, the solid such-ness of his factual compassion rattling me like a set of dice in the hands of a nervous gambler. Those weeks of undirected anger in the aftermath of our fierce cold war, the subsequent months of introspection and blinding uncertainty which lead only to entire years of a spiteful, harrowing toil undertaken mainly to prove him wrong, all founded on a false pretense?

"So you're saying I heard you wrong? Bullshit. I will never forget what you said to me. It was the only argument we ever had."

"It's not so much that you heard me wrong," he said, lighting a joint he had pulled from his front pocket and opening another beer.

"It's not that you heard me wrong. It's that you didn't know what you should have been listening for." At this, I involuntarily made the sound one makes when they're dismissing another. A laugh when one can't be bothered to laugh.

"Say what you mean, Yoda."

He nodded solemnly and seemed to disappear inwardly toward the depths of his self, searching for the words, just as he had done earlier when trying to convey to me that his dog seemed estranged. Eventually, he returned to the surface, clutching a treasure.

"What I mean is, memorizing the writers' handbook doesn't make you a writer. It makes you a specialist, and it puts you in a class with people who were given the same training. You all share the same view from the same room." He looked at me with a modicum of pain in his eyes and tensed his shoulders as if half expecting to see me die and half expecting to see me try to kill him, but I made no move. He continued.

"See, the thing is, you looked like a writer, and you sounded like a writer, and you even wrote like a writer, but you refused to acknowledge the soul that makes a writer an *actual* writer. Do you understand?" I could do nothing but frown and shrug and shake my head in disbelief, feebly attempting to convince him that I didn't care, that nothing could hurt me anymore, but that wasn't true. Something resounded so completely that my eyes actually began welling up. Fires were being set under my feet.

"The things you wrote were heavy, and a talent was there, but inside of those things, your true self was nowhere to be found, the thing that could have made you special. You were not present." He took a drag of his joint and a swig of beer. "Yes, you used large words. I'll give you that. And you were very meticulous in where you used them, but all those characteristics of 'your style,'" he made air quotes as he spoke the last two words, "were distractions. They got people to look away from the fact that there was no soul in your work. Nothing dove in. No one was engaged. I mean, it made for an interesting read, and if put to music you could even sell it. But in my opinion it just never got to the point. People will voluntarily enter mazes, but only because they believe they'll eventually get out. I personally could not get out. You would give it to me to read and I'd just get trapped. I would become uncertain and double back again, and at the end I took nothing away except: "Wow. That maze was hard." I wanted to earn something from you. I wanted to earn a connection to you through it, and I couldn't. Nothing you wrote ever touched my heart because it never touched yours."

"And it's because you thought too much and you felt too little. Your writing was aimed at the head. Which isn't a *bad* thing, but anyone can do that if they put in time. I only say this because I genuinely believe I actually knew you back then. Not the *you* you showed other people. The *you* before you became what you thought you wanted to be. We had a connection from the moment we met that you seemed to be ashamed to acknowledge." I nodded and tried to swallow the knot that was forming in my throat.

"It's okay. I know Frank made it very hard. I just think that what makes someone a writer is how well they know truth *and* how well they love beauty. You actually did the opposite. You just kind of used crazy metaphors to hide insults and glorify your own weaknesses and you pretended that life was out to get you and you made excuses for the shitty things you did to other people. But someone would have to know you like I did to see that you were secretly asking for forgiveness. For help." Denying him the right to present all evidence would be to deny the deep rumble that guided my steps all these years. This was my atonement. It would be slow and thorough and I would abide.

"When you lost Claire, I thought you would come back with the most honest stuff you were capable of writing. You could have turned that into the most important lesson of your life. But you never learn. Instead, you buried your heart even further beneath these elaborate symbols, and it was like, Jesus Christ, give me a fucking break. You were so afraid to be honest with yourself. You completely fucked her up, Raymond. *Completely* fucked her up. And I know because I was there the night she left. I sat with her while she wept. I talked to her and I closed that book for you. I didn't just hang up on her. I didn't discard her like you did. You didn't deserve her." Again, Evan swiped his finger across the air as if he were tossing aside a piece of paper on a desk. "And you wouldn't acknowledge it. Instead, you partnered with that enormous ego of yours and you wasted real inspiration to maintain the image of a writer you gave yourself when you were like seventeen and I knew that was dishonest. So, no, I didn't want you to stop writing. I wanted you to let out the writer inside of you instead of acting like the ones you saw out in front."

"I never had an ego, Evan. I never thought I was better than anyone. I just knew I saw things differently than others and I had a different way of saying it. Not better. Just *different*. That's all. It's not egotistical to be confident."

Evan smiled peacefully. "Oh, really, RAY GOLDMAN? You didn't think you were above anybody?" My soul reeled as the dangerous implications of a *stage name* set in. I had never seen it like that before. Evan's revealing light was seeping through a crack.

"It's not even that. You're misunderstanding the concept of an ego. I don't mean like a Kanye West or that shithead with the furry hat that fucks troubled women. That's just the way certain people behave when their ego has them in its grips. This is more fundamental, further down the rabbit hole. By 'ego' I mean the idea of who you are. What you see in your head when you hear your own name."

CHAPTER TWENTY-TWO

AMONTH AFTER THE SHOW, I RECEIVED a call from the head of an independent label based out of Los Angeles, California called Elegy Records. They said Matt had sent them a copy of my demo. They said I would make a perfect addition to their roster. They said they would give me a budget of ten thousand dollars to record a full-length record as long as I could assure them that I would tour for at least fifteen weeks out of the year, and they said that what I didn't spend on production was mine to keep in addition to a five thousand–dollar signing bonus, which was recoupable from the merchandise I sold on tour. The 5k alone was more money than I ever knew existed in the world, but the fact that I would record my own songs meant that the 10k was also mine to keep. So as the owner of the label explained the terms and conditions, my mind left the earth on a magic carpet made of cash. I saw myself acquiring, conquering, hoarding, reaping, and, most importantly, controlling. I was not in the hands of fate, nor vulnerable to the precocious currents of time. I would eat when hungry. I would drink when dry. My needs that had been slowly fulfilled over time would be replaced by wants that were met immediately. I had domination over the fantastic territory of my childhood dreams, and that child answered for me before my adult mind could shut its mouth.

"Yes. Absolutely. I will do anything," I told the label's owner at the end of our phone call.

Of course, there were things that my inner child did not take into consideration, but being rational was not the duty of the inner child. It was there only to answer the call that an adult who has been deafened by obligation might not hear. The adult me was enrolled in college, while the child me whimsically strummed a guitar. The adult me had a hardworking father who was paying for my education, while the child me had a father who brought home flat vinyl circles into which were carved the voices of different gods. The adult me had made a commitment to a beautiful girl, while the child me was loved by all. The adult me had no time. The child me had eternity. The call was too loud, and it rendered the adult me inconsequential. I needed to break the news to Claire.

After her classes that Friday, Claire would, as she had been doing recently, arrive at my house with a travel bag. She spent Monday through Friday in her dorm room focused solely on her studies, but she became a temporary roommate to me, Frank, and Evan on Saturdays and Sundays, and her presence was a much needed change of scenery. She and I were young enough to still be excited about conjugal visits, and Evan and Frank welcomed the sight of a stunningly beautiful art student lounging in her underwear on the couch, smoking pot, and screaming at the football game. She was just tomboyish enough to feel unashamed about shotgunning beer or contributing to the crass conversations of my circle of friends, but when we were alone, that masculine camaraderie transformed into an unthinkable elegance and sexual confidence. She was so far out of my league I could only hope to hold onto her heart for a few moments before I was thrown from it like a rider on a wild horse. After she arrived, undressed, fucked me, dressed, made a drink, and put on a Modest Mouse record, she sat down at the foot of my bed and asked what was distracting me.

"I have some news you're not going to be happy about."

She bowed her head and took a deep breath. "I can handle it. Did you meet someone?"

"No, no. It's not about us. It's about me. I…" I paused as I became aware of a sudden shame dissolving into my enthusiasm. "I got a call from a record label in California. The one Matt Skiba took my tape to. They want to sign me. They want to give me a record deal." Claire looked up at me, her eyes wide, her beautiful, thin, elfin lips pulled tight against her pronounced cheekbones.

"RAYMOND!" she screamed, and leapt up. "Why would you assume I wouldn't love this news?" She held my face in her hands and kissed me.

"Because it means I have to leave. Often. And for a while."

"So?"

"Our relationship is going to become long distance."

"So?"

"You'll wait for me?"

"I will fucking wait right here in this very spot for you," she said as she slapped the mattress. "In this bed. In my underwear. For all time."

"What if you meet someone else?"

"There is no one else, Raymond. I love you alone for as long as you will let me." I was astonished. What had I done to convince this girl that I was worth waiting for? What right did I have being so firmly lodged in her loving gaze?

"You love me?" I asked, as excited as I was confused.

"Yes. I think I do." She kissed me again.

"Maybe you think too much," I said smiling, taking her drink out of her hand and throwing half of it back like a pill. "I'm a mess."

"No, you are not! You want people to believe you are, but you ain't." She took her drink back. "You're just a little baby."

I laughed out loud as she wrapped her arms around me. "My little baby!" she yelled, "My little baby with his bottle and his little acoustic rattle! Gonna crawl around the world singin' his little songs!"

"You should move in," I said. "Wait right here for me in your underwear."

"Not this exact pair, right? I can change every morning?"

"If you insist."

"I do." She hugged me hard and was moved in by the next week.

To my surprise, my father was also incredibly supportive of my decision to drop out of school to pursue this *career* in music, assuring me that "knowledge will be there when you want it, but demand for your talent will not." So, for the second time in my life, I left my classes unfinished at the behest of my father and when I received word that withdrawal was official, I couldn't help but feel that life wouldn't ever let me finish what I'd started. My mother enthusiastically cosigned on a loan for a mini van, which also was surprising considering it was a vessel that had the sole purpose of hastily guiding her only son into a world she couldn't inhabit. But perhaps both of my parents knew they couldn't impede the progress of destiny on its way to fulfillment; that by nurturing the growth of their seed rather than opposing it, they would be allowed remote vision through it. My parents had lived in the same suburban house my entire life because it was modified to accommodate the needs of Lilly, and they never traveled because she was too delicate to disturb. Their lives were spent in the nest caring for an egg that would never hatch, and through me, all three of them—especially my sister—had a way to participate both in and above the world. I was an extension of their own senses into a realm they could never venture, and as long as I returned to tell them about it, they were given a chance to know the unknown through me. After a few more correspondences with the label, my first tour was booked. With Frank in tow as my tour manager, I left home for the sake of warfare on March 20th, 2002 as the direct support for Alkaline Trio. The door closed behind me.

That first month of tour was a poisoned land upon which nothing could be built, but seeing only my goal of fame and nothing else, I went above and beyond what was required of me by the label—and Frank stayed with me every step of the way. We toured relentlessly after that run with Alkaline Trio ended, missing holidays, weddings, anniversaries, deaths, and births. Those rituals and routines belonged to a species of life that lived on an alien planet. My home was the road now, and my art was my job. Eddie, Aaron, Claire, they couldn't understand what it was like where I wandered. They reported to bosses and were given tasks to complete. My only obligation was to my heart.

The first year I struggled against impossible odds to break any ground at all, with the universe throwing everything at me, night after night, city after city. But I would not fail. In spite of a cruel God, I pressed on. I cursed him every morning that I awoke on the hardwood floors of kind strangers' houses, and every night before I fell asleep sitting upright in the van waiting for a Wal-Mart to open. I cursed him as I was forced to steal gas to get to the next town or steal groceries to stave off hunger. I mother-fucked our Lord and Savior every single time I iced a broken finger after a bar fight and each time I took the stage in front of a half-empty room. Engines failed, tires blew, batteries died, strings broke, voices cracked, tempers flared, fists flew, blood spilled, Claire suffered, money vanished, sleep never came. The debut record put out through Elegy that I recorded in two weeks of off time barely made a ripple in the scene. People were simply not responding to my music. I had opened tours for Chamberlain and Lucero. I had headlined tours over upcoming acts like Frank Turner and Dallas Green, but nothing worked. No breaks came. And though I pressed on, I became acutely aware of a voice in my head that whispered tales of failure—and it only grew louder with every poorly attended show. Maybe I never should have left school. Maybe I never should have left home. The universe was a swamp and God was a rabid dog. He was against me now just as he had always been against me. *Fuck him*, I thought, and after being booed off the stage at a festival in Chicago, I put whatever measly crumbs that were left of my faith on the heap of trash alongside my degree and my relationships and vowed to do it alone. And so I did. What those with understanding might have seen as a sign to change direction, I took as a chance to challenge fate by moving forward. I was too stupid to know better, and too inexperienced to recognize defeat.

In the second year of maniacal touring, the course of my ship began to change significantly, mainly due to the development of the internet, which altered paradigms of promotion and the scope of exposure to new audiences. In its early stages, it was just an enormous chat room in which I could find like-minded people to talk about music or places I could go to look at pictures of girls doing weird shit with their holes while my roommates were out. But now that I was on the road, Frank discovered that it could be used to serve our careers, and over a few weeks he taught me simple methods to make new fans. The word-of-mouth means of sharing information was intensified. The more mouths you had working for you, the louder your voice, and the further it could travel. It took my life and career as an artist out of the hands of the higher ups at the record label and gave a little of it back to me. Plus, having already mastered the do-it-yourself lifestyle in my first year on the road, it took no effort at all to matriculate into a culture dominated by the self. I could self-record with a few digital amps, program drums on a computer, and self-promote on MySpace.

There was no longer a need to print flyers and hand them out in the freezing cold or stay up all night burning CDs to sell under the radar of the label in order to actually have some pocket money for dinner. Frank taught himself web design, built a site devoted to my music, and by the first day over five hundred people had looked at my tour dates. I learned how to upload live recordings, and *literally* overnight people learned my words and could be heard singing along as I played. I could have easily dismissed all this new technology as a purist believing that only blood, sweat, and tears can alter a man's lot in life. But why? Evolution was occurring. The rules of the world as we knew it were shifting in mysterious ways, and if I didn't evolve with it, what kind of animal would I be?

Ticket sales increased. Record sales spiked. By late 2004, I had over one hundred thousand friends on MySpace and began touring overseas. That was also around the time that Dimebag Darrell died, shot by a disturbed fan, which forced most of the music community to realize just how vulnerable performers can be up there on stage, but I feared nothing and would fill any space left vacant by those who were discouraged by death. American kids with beards and flannel shirts now recognized me in public and gave me free cigarettes and bought me drinks. People wanted my autograph. I was getting blowjobs from girls with real tattoos on their fake tits while Claire went to classes in another time zone. I was making enough to sleep in hotels, but we never slept because the girls with the fake tits and their friends with beards and flannels always brought us free cocaine. I would go four or five days without talking to anyone from back home. I tore through life like a storm with claws, gluttonously absorbing experience after experience after experience, annihilating time itself and leaving it in shambles from my wake. A string of nights a thousand miles long tailing me like the train of a wedding gown. I put on fifty pounds and began covering my body in meaningless tattoos—

souvenirs from the locals of the towns Frank and I had plundered. The haze of chemicals and fatuous approval was so thick that I could no longer differentiate between right and wrong. I began negotiating with my own soul, convincing myself that the meaning of life was to sample every fruit, no matter how low-hanging. I told my heart that there were things you do *to* other women and things you do *with* other women, and that as long as Claire was the only woman I did things *with* any sexual act was more of a casual and meaningless exchange of favors. *Phrasing was everything.* There were so many loopholes around promiscuity and addiction that sin itself became a vacuous notion and virtue was a grail unavailable to us pitiful humans. These were the spoils of all my hard work. I had earned the right to flaunt honor. The sex, the alcohol, the applause, the attention, the admiration, these things were mine now. Ray fucking Goldman. The grotesque. The lonely. The loved.

Frank, too, found clever ways to capitalize on my sudden success, abandoning his art entirely and turning himself into what would come to be known as an internet "celebrity." Girls had always found him handsome and charming when they met him in person, and with us constantly on the move now it was easier to facilitate meetings with women he had up until that point only chatted with online, but when he began his own channel on a website called YouTube in 2005 where he did nothing more than film himself talking about his life on the road (never once mentioning who he was working for), his *stardom* skyrocketed, his website generating tens of thousands of hits monthly. I was dumbfounded. While I had spent years trying to discover what it was that people wanted from my music, Frank had given them nothing more than himself and he met no resistance in the process. He was tasting immortality and it was simultaneously the most honest act and egomaniacal farce I had ever seen. Girls fawned over him more than they did me. They were going to *my* shows and asking for *his* autograph.

It became very obvious very quickly that his preternatural ability to sense an opportunity for self-aggrandizement, mixed with his shameless bolstering, was the precise cocktail for fame and he would achieve it by doing nothing other than trying to *become* famous. He had no service to provide, no talent to share. It was an impossible concept, ouroboros in nature, and though I again found myself resentful of the opportunistic makeup of it all, the commodity he made out of himself put bodies in the rooms where I played my guitar. It brought new fans into the venues, and those new fans were likely to buy my record. So what right did I have to complain? I was the fortunate victim of Frank Qynn's self-serving generosity, a confounding phenomenon that had rendered me inert since the moment I shook his hand.

CHAPTER TWENTY-THREE

I. THAT CRUDE LETTER. THAT CRUEL WORD.
The flimsy box carrying all we knew of the world since the whole world began. A blind tyrant, both ever watchful and ever judged, stitched carefully onto a moth-eaten flag and brazenly draped over the balconies that lined the streets down which life inexorably marches. The *I* and everything it stood for was a fate as shaky as the landscape from which it sprung, and though it often felt as if it belonged to me, it only seemed that way because the *I* allowed me to believe I was in charge. Truthfully, it was the *I* that fed me. It nourished and clothed and advised me. It found me, broke me, lifted me up, showed me love, and then broke me again. It spoke to me as I slept, slithering into my brain like a beautiful woman into a warm bath, whispering of its loyalty so that I would awake drenched in gluttonous pride. It was wider than the universe and small enough to move in my blood. It reached in toward and spread out from absolute nothingness. It *was* that nothingness. It experimented with its own forms, toying with truth in a field set apart from time, privately un- and redoing itself, nimbly struggling against the waning patience of the unamused. My entire world was in that letter, all my sadness, all my jealousy, all my guilt, and all my strength. A series of pictures flashed inside

of me, as vivid as if they were before my eyes. A marble statue moving clumsily upward toward the crest of an endless mountain, high above the clouds, now miles above the ground where I had seen him last but still nowhere near where he could rest. Parts of his body were clearly defined but the potential of true beauty was offset by crude angles jutting in all directions from his hands and face. He was unfinished but familiar. I watched as he stumbled again and again, pathetic and tired and hopeless at the end of the whip of the unsympathetic *I*.

"That *I* inside of you?" Evan said after what felt like an eternity. "That person you see when you hear your name? He's an entirely separate thing from you. He might have some of the same features in common, but he's not you. I mean, it's the product of a process, but it started with kind of your own personal big bang," he said, looking up into the sky. "The moment you saw who you wanted to be as something different from who you already were, a fucking galaxy of possibilities exploded into being. It's like we all start off as this perfect thing that just is. And we're there, chilling. Immortal. Perfectly happy, playing with a fucking stick or whatever. But then, someone makes fun of us in school or breaks our hearts and we get this crazy idea that if we were someone else everyone would be happy, and instantly a line is drawn through the field of time that goes directly to death and the version of you that you think you'd rather be just starts walking it because it has nowhere else to go now except forward. It's like a mother bird kicking the baby bird out of the nest, and now that scared little thing has to make its way in the world because it can't possibly go back. The nest, the height it came from, is unreachable. But the thing is, you are not only the bird, you are also the mother and the spirit that watches over both, the being that sees this all taking place. We forget that. We forget that we expelled ourselves from our own place of safety and happiness for whatever stupid reason. Some think it's because we were curious, some think we were too content, others think it's because we couldn't give anything back to the nest that gave us so much and we felt guilty about not earning our keep. Whatever. It's not important why we did it, what matters is that we did it. So now, there's this other part of us walking down the path of life through time toward death, and the memory of our mother self becomes foggier and foggier until eventually it disappears almost completely and we find ourselves truly alone. So, to deal with our loneliness, we summon our spirit to accompany us on the journey and together we do everything we can to distract us from that inevitable death that we brought on ourselves. But the *you* that's out there walking that line is not who you really are. Well, it is, it's a part of you, but it's the dark part. The mortal part. And after a few years of suffering, it becomes so resentful of the immortal part of itself that put it down on that earthly path that it almost detaches entirely. It denies its mother, and there aren't three parts to the whole anymore, there are just two separate parts connected by this ever-thinning bridge of spirit. Some call that bridge faith, but you can call it whatever the fuck you want." I saw Sophia with my mind's eye. "It's fun down here. Can't argue that."

"Well yeah, because that's all we know. It's what we tell ourselves. But it's a lie. Your senses tell you only what you're willing to accept in order to fend off death a little longer. It tells you you're a victim because if you believe that you're a victim, you fight against the people that threaten to bring death. But you're not the victim, you're the cause. You kicked yourself out of the nest. And you're not a fighter either." I thought back to Frank, and to how, even as I watched the dark blood drip out of me and back into the earth in the instant before his foot cracked my rib, I could not muster up the desire needed to hit back. I never really cared about anything enough to fight for it. Not even myself.

"Matter of fact?" he said, wagging his finger at me somewhat drunkenly. "You're not even a real drinker. You secretly hate it because every time you drink, it reminds you that you have no idea how to let go and just be without it." He laughed to himself now and watched me intently for a reassuring smirk that I thought he was right, which I couldn't help but give him.

"I knew it! But, see, if you admit that, then what happens to that guy out there on that stage? You think Ray Goldman is willing to say that after all this, that he loves the nest more? Fuck no. If he did, he would have to surrender everything he knows. He would have to forfeit his self. He would have to let go of all the stuff he gathered as he walked the earth and that would make him look weak and hypocritical and he can't do that because how he is seen is all he has. And what he actually *is* is too out of reach. Too high up. Too long ago. And if you admit you want to go back to where you started, where will your fans go? Where will your music come from? You don't want to go back to the nest. You love the attention you've gotten while walking through life way too much. So you let that little driving force keep you alive, fighting off death any way you can, forgetting it comes for us all." Evan handed me another beer. I opened it and took a small, disingenuous sip.

"And what's so unfortunate about your situation, is that your ego wasn't just a little voice, it was a corporeal form that lived in our house. That angry narcissist was reaffirming every single doubt you had, and moving you further away from your source because you were his ticket." I thought of shaking Frank's hand for the first time at Aaron's party. How uncertain it made me, how guilty and scared and alone. "If you weren't *you*, then who could *he* be? He ruined you. He made you so old in your youth. It was terrible to watch. Poor you. The inside of your head must have looked like a fucking typhoon. And poor Frank." He took a mouthful of beer to calm himself down after briefly yielding to thoughts that would have made a lesser man crazed with anger.

"Poor Frank?" I exclaimed in disbelief. It was the first sound I had made in a while. It came without warning from somewhere up ahead, somewhere I hadn't been keeping an eye on. "Fuck that. I haven't even told you the worst of it. He beat the shit out of me one night on tour."

"Doesn't matter. Forgive him. Listen," he said effortlessly, zipping his hand across the air between us, again clearing the slate. The ease with which he dismissed the idea of holding onto any pain was remarkable. It was almost as if pain itself wasn't real. And yet it seemed to be the most natural thing he could have done. Evan didn't just act as if forgiving Frank was the simplest thing in the world, he knew it to be so. He moved onto the next picture of an arrow in flight.

"The thing is, none of the shit that *that* version of us experiences is real. Nothing. It's real to a version of ourselves, but when you pull your awareness back a bit, when that spirit wrests itself away from you and back toward the direction of the source, it becomes obvious how little most things matter to the big picture. I see that now. I've always had a feeling, but now I've pulled back, and I know it. But, still, because we are all here on this road, we will suffer and die defending the ideas we give ourselves. Like we are what *is* and we have to protect ourselves from what *is not*. We fight. And what if realizing that on your own ends up being the most liberating epiphany you could ever have instead of the most terrifying thought?

What if I thought, acknowledging the old acquaintance that was that phrase.

Evan lit another joint with urgency, trembling with excitement like a horse at the gate. "It sounds stupid, and I know you're gonna fight me on this because you love your job and you're proud of all you've done and being a writer is all you've ever wanted to be, but consider it. What if it *was* all wrong? What if—instead of life being this relentless lurch forward through heartache—we could make it a series of lessons that teach us how to get back to that place we kicked ourselves out of? I mean, the deed is done. You made the decision to be something else at some point in your life and it wasn't your fault. You had no idea how much power you had in your hands, particularly if the decision was made when you were just a baby and your mom, I don't know, took her titty away a little too soon. But what if you can undo it? What if we can undo all the universes of options that opened up every single time you lied to yourself about who you are and learn how to get back home? What if you could abandon the *I*?

What if.

Evan looked out where the hills should be, under all the darkness, and he pulled a long deep drag from his smoldering joint. As he did, the cherry lit up the entire night. I saw his face and his dark wild eyes and the water tumbling from an iron fountain at the base of a wave of rock that rose slowly and leaned toward the black and white shards of a vast canyon, and before the bright red light dwindled into a low orange the color of an infant dawn, I wondered if the night briefly saw me too.

"I think maybe you have the wrong idea of me," I said, though not so much out of concern as out of the desire to say anything at all. What I meant or hoped to gain was irrelevant because I had no idea what I believed anymore. A *wrong idea* seemed like a useless term. According to Evan, all ideas were wrong and there was no shelf upon which I could put any new fact. It would go on the floor in a new pile to be sorted through later. "You've seen the things I've written," I said. "You told me you've read my lyrics. How can you not see that I, too, believe this all means nothing? I'm, like, the biggest proponent of the inconsequentiality of this all. I know full well that no matter what we do, we end up in the ground at the same depth as the people that do nothing good at all." The soothing fire of intoxication raced through my body and I could feel the poet in me emerge from the clear flames. "I get that. Life has never done any of us any good, so I don't think its fair to be lumping me in with people that don't get it. You're preaching to the choir when you talk about meaninglessness."

Maybe I really wanted Evan to tell me how wrong I had been and steer me in a new direction. Maybe I wasn't looking to argue my nihilism as much as I was offering up to the retired tinkerer a grand misconception in the desperate hopes he could now fix what I had thrown away. Evan hung his head and shook it slowly as if he had been trying for hours to give instructions to someone who didn't speak the same language.

"No, you definitely do not get it. Meaninglessness and impermanence are not the same thing. Look. I know you make a living off of what you've written and the strange way you see things, but stop standing there for just a minute. Try it. Stop giving me proof that you are who you say you are or building a case for the authenticity of *you*. Ignore your *self*. It's not real, Raymond. It's a hologram and there is no intrinsic value to the things that make up this image. But if you convince yourself there is, if you mistake the map for the terrain and turn those little bouts of self-pity into your whole life, which, judging by your songs, you have definitely done, then yes life will appear random and cruel and the universe will work against you because you are quietly, secretly begging it to reinforce who you are. You're convinced you need pain to create so it gives you what you ask for whether you like it or not. But there is so much light outside of that crowded, dirty house your ego keeps you trapped in. Life is not the abyss you keep talking about in your lyrics. Only your version of it. You talk about *the void* more than Anthony Kiedis talks about California. I get it. Your fans get it. You need a new trick. A new outlook could serve you well." He flashed a smile.

"So what are you even telling me to do? Be friendlier? Give to charity? Go to church? I don't get it."

"Not necessarily, selfish acts of kindness are just a different kind of ego trip. It's sneakier and less obvious, but it's the same thing. People that are publicly virtuous want to be recognized for being nice the way models want to be recognized for being good looking. It's still narcissism. Just more subtle."

"My friend Ray," Frank loudly declared as he stood on his chair "is going to play for awla you drunks."

"You really think that this little talk is going to convince me to give up all I know? Just start over? I've worked way too hard."

"Well, no. You don't have to burn it all in one night, but you can at least start down a path toward that light. Toward remembering god."

I cringed and grew uncomfortable. "Evan," I said. "Really? Are you doing mission work or something? This is starting to sound like a sales pitch."

"Relax for a second." Evan looked upset for the first time all night, as if I had disparaged a member of his family. "You have no idea what I mean when I say 'god.' I don't mean a dude on a fuckin' cloud answering letters and judging souls or any of that bullshit. That's what you think it means because you heard about him from the church who has it all wrong."

"So, *you* know more about God than the church, and *my* ego is out of control?"

"First of all, I'm telling you your ego is *in* control and that's the problem—and second of all, yes, I do know more than the church, but the church is a whole other thing." Evan took a pull off the bottle of Scotch and chased it back with a swig of beer. "The church is just another result of a massive misunderstanding. But when I referred to 'God' I meant, and I still mean, 'God' as an intelligence, or a passion. The something inside of us that knows everything. I wish there was another word for it, but there isn't. So we all call it god, which is too bad because the true, original meaning has been so fucking diluted. But whatever, doesn't matter. Words don't matter. Call it fucking Don for all I care. I'm just trying to make the disclaimer that I'm not talking about the Church God or the Republican God. I'm talking about Jesus's god. Buddha's god. The god that showed up inside of Da Vinci and Mozart and Newton and Shakespeare and Pythagoras and Einstein and Ghandi and the Dali Lama, versions one through fourteen and fourteen through one zillion, and Stephen Hawking and Steve Jobs and every other person on earth that never even knew they were also god. *That* is the god I'm talking about. That bolt of inspiration. As a writer, it's the feeling you get when you find *the word*. When you play the guitar, god is the thing that helps you a call a melody out of nowhere. When Frank would paint or draw, it was that nudge that guided his hand. By the way, is he still drawing? He was a rare talent."

"Nope. He stopped as soon as we started touring full time."

"That's a real shame. Okay, but anyways, what I'm saying is that the term god just refers to the consciousness that is the cause of all and only great things. And if they don't seem great at the moment, it's only because *you* insisted on living down here in the field of time. So don't complain that you now may have to exercise a little fucking patience when waiting for meaning to appear.

The open seat behind Hannah on the first day of middle school. Professor Tiller's numerical oversight. A pamphlet blown up against the fence.

Evan was at the height of his enthusiasm now. His eyes were darts and his body was speaking hundreds of languages at once, all telling the same story. As he did so, I wondered what else might have been lightly peppered into the joint he was smoking. "Do you get me?" He went on. "I know you have achieved some moderate fame sculpting works of art out of the piles of shit you've subconsciously acquired as your medium, but that's because you work harder than anyone I've ever known and people appreciate that. But are you really fulfilled? Are you really alive? Don't you feel like you've done all you can do with it? When something becomes truly powerful it becomes something else, and I can't help but get the feeling you're stuck on repeat in an early stage of *something-ness*. I've followed your career online a little bit over the past few years. I've read about the fights, the DWIs, the drug charges that your PR manages to get overturned. I've also read your lyrics, and if I can be honest, it seems like you're just finding newer ways to say old things. I worry about you. You can get yourself out of this cycle of constant death and suffering, Raymond. But not if you insist on bringing Ray with you."

He laid back against the chair and crossed his feet and I laid back against mine, looking out into the swelling night. He fell silent.

"But I have become powerful enough to become something else. I'm selling more records than ever, I'm riding in a bus playing to thousands of people a night where I used to drive a minivan and play to ten. I have a house now. A car. A wife. A fucking water bed. Six-year-old me would shit himself if he knew that one day he'd be sleeping in his own water bed. I've achieved the success I have wanted since I picked up a guitar."

"Cobain might have said the same thing once."

I let that settle in. "Okay so where was this person when we lived together? You were always so quiet and weird and now you hit me with this indictment as if you were observing an animal from a distance and keeping notes on me the whole time. Why didn't we have this talk earlier?" Evan took another drag off his joint.

"Well firstly, I tried once but I apparently wounded your pride so thoroughly that you had 'Ray Goldman' shut me out of your life until just now. Secondly, Frank was an impressive force in that house and I hadn't really found enough conviction to know how to be honest in his presence."

"I can see that."

"But, since I try to find a lesson in everything, I realize now that I was meditating to learn patience and he made that apartment a state of the art facility to test my new skills in. His ego, his pride, his insecurity, his opportunism." Another drag. "He was a master of all those vices, and if I could learn to forgive them and love him in spite of them, I could uncover who I really was. Unfortunately we all moved out before I ever had the chance to. But Frank is one of the best teachers you will ever have, Raymond. Don't waste his lessons like you wasted Claire's. Things like that rarely happen twice. Learn from him while he still hates you enough to teach you the things you need to know."

CHAPTER TWENTY-FOUR

SINCE I HADN'T SPOKEN TO HER IN OVER two weeks, it came as no surprise to me that Claire had moved out of my apartment by the time I returned home from tour in the summer of 2005. Perhaps if I had actually used the venue's pay phone booths to call her and listen to the things she had to say instead of just visiting them briefly for clandestine sexual trists with girls I had met at my shows, she would have at least left a note. But there was nothing. She had vanished as if never there at all, leaving no trace of her beauty in my selfish heart. This, of course, was no fault of her own. Her honest young love never stood a chance against the behemoth of debauchery that a young man, given sudden success, finds awakened in his ancient soul. The last time we had spoken, she wept deeply as I paced in front of a pay phone outside of a Shell station off the I-10. If I wanted to, I could picture her alone in our room across from Evan's sitting on the corner of my bed wearing one of the plaid shirts I had given her with giant tears pouring out from under her red glasses, but I didn't want to. What I could actually see in real life was Frank waving his hands and pointing at his watch through the window.

"Raymond. Please," she said with a unique and almost holy longing in her voice. "I don't need you to come home. I just need to know that you remember me. You haven't called me in a week, I miss your voice, I'm so lonely here."

"Bullshit. You want me to give this up because you resent me. You are unhappy with your own life and you're taking it out on me because I refuse to be unhappy with you. I didn't make you move in with me. I didn't ask you to fall in love."

"No. No. No," she sobbed. "That's not true. I just need to feel like I'm close to you. Just to feel *like* it. I know we can't be it. But lie to me. Anything. Just make me believe you're coming back to me. I will wait forever if I believe that. I will settle for faith, Raymond. I don't need proof. Just faith." More sobbing. Desperate, breathless, sobbing.

And as she wept—her voice shaking with more genuine pain than anyone should ever be possessive of—I detached. Was Evan going to move out? It was pretty obvious I didn't want him in the house anymore after realizing how unnecessarily cruel and jealous he was capable of being. If he stayed it would simply be too uncomfortable to act natural. I should open the set with a new song tonight. A beer would be so fucking good right now. I think there are some in the cooler in the van. There definitely were. There's no way Chet would not have left any behind. How many T-shirts would I sell at the shows in Florida? Probably a lot. It was summer and I had printed some thin tanks tops this time around. I looked at Frank and shrugged, as if to say I had no idea what was going on in this baseless, illusory world of scorned women, but I knew. I had run out of fantasies and whatever was left in the hive they abandoned was off limits to her heart.

Hanging up the phone on her just happened. I didn't even know I was going to do it. My right hand just sort of burst away from my ear and the next thing I knew, the black plastic was hanging on the grey metal and her voice was lost to me for good, back on the pile with the rest. In mid-sentence, I hung up the phone and leapt proudly back into a chasm from which I would never truly return. I didn't even remember it happening. *Oh well*, I thought. *It had been too late for too long. Claire loved a devil.*

Once back in the front seat of the minivan, Chet, Frank, Cube, and I got onto the I-75 and headed south toward Orlando. The sun was shining and the specific Florida foliage was still new enough to me to seem exotic, the palm trees and swamplands reminding me of a trip to my uncle's house with my parents. Lilly wasn't born yet, so I must have been around three or four. My uncle taught me to swear on that visit. He sat me on the table and got me to call my mother, his own sister, a "bitch." It took some urging, but when I finally spit it out, everyone laughed. It was one of my earliest memories...

"I'm a free man, boys." I said, looking back over the headrest of my seat. Chet looked puzzled.

"Weren't you a free man when I caught you getting jerked off on this seat bench a few nights ago?"

"No, Chet. I was not. But now I am." I faced forward and dipped my hand into a bag of chips I bought.

"This is awesome," Frank said, reaching his hand into my bag without taking his eyes off the road. "You can finally be my wingman." Now, with his mouth full: "She was always so rude to me." At this, Chet cackled an incredulous laugh from the back of the van.

"Are you fucking kidding me?" I looked back and forth between he and Frank, somewhat confused by the way their reactions were unfolding. "If she was rude to you it's because you're the world's biggest cocksucker. Claire was *the* sweetest girl I've ever met. If you're single now, Ray, I'm going to fucking marry her. Hope you don't mind. Actually, I don't care if you mind. She's not yours anymore."

"Okay. Stop," I said. "I don't want to shit talk her or start to regret my decision. I'm just saying, we broke up." At that moment, it dawned on me that neither of us had actually made a decision to formally break up, it was just sort of implied through the symbol of the dial tone. Though it would probably be understood that we were through, I never actually let her finish speaking. She needed to talk to me, to find closure, and my entire being abruptly pulled out of the conversation because I was, what? Too bored to continue? Too scared to hear what she needed to say? It was the most underhanded, cowardly thing I could have done. I turned back around and sat quietly, staring out the windshield at the road. The road that unflinchingly connected and divided everything in the world. The road that receded as I approached and approached as I receded. The road that would go on alongside of me at any speed I chose and upon which a thing and its opposite could exist, both simultaneously and eternally.

"Either way, you'll be better off, man," Frank said.

"No. She'll be better off, man," Chet said, childishly mimicking Frank.

Cube giggled quietly.

The show in Orlando was one of the best of that tour. I was direct support for Ryan Adams that month, and since his fans alone were enough to fill most venues, most of the time I was playing in front of people that had never even heard of me. But those that were unfamiliar responded well to the new sound I had to offer them. Considering it was just me and an acoustic guitar up there for a half hour, there was no heckling. No bottle throwing. I was sometimes selling over a grand in merchandise a night and the record I had put out was moving so fast I had to have the label ship more out to me on a few occasions. I had money in my pocket like I had never seen and for the first time ever I was able to pay Chet and Frank and Cube well enough to cover their rent for the months they spent on the road. It felt incredible to be able to nurture those I cared about, particularly myself.

After we were loaded out and all packed up, the four of us walked out to our van and pulled up behind a black Mercedes that was sitting in the street. The car belonged to a guy Chet had met at the bar. After purchasing white drugs from him, Chet got us all invited to a party at a house that belonged to a wealthy client of the dealer, though we were not told whom specifically. Within twenty minutes, we were being let in through a gate that opened automatically once my name was said into an intercom. We parked the dirty black van in a spot next to a Porsche, huddled around the duffel bag of cocaine that Chet held out, and went inside to begin the game.

The four of us split up as soon as we entered, each of us following a different star that our coke highs shined above us. As I waded through the crowd and approached the bar to order a drink, I began to wonder why there were so many empty beer bottles lying around. Wasn't there a maid for stuff like this? It looked like the party had been going on for a century. I was in a house worth more than I could dream about and they couldn't be bothered to clean these up…and what is with the THOUSANDS of cigarette butts that overflowed the twenty or thirty ashtrays placed in windowsills and on top of arcade game consoles? What the fuck? Is that a pile of chocolate fountains covered in mold on a table in a forgotten corner? Like, a whole PILE OF CHOCOLATE FOUNTAINS?! What was going on here? I looked quickly to my right at the dirty bong tipped over in front of a stained microsuede couch that sat underneath a framed platinum record hanging crookedly between two wall-sized windows. Crooked? Who achieves that success and allows the proof to hang crooked in a house full of beautiful guests? Intrigued beyond all measure I quickly walked over to it.

This Platinum Record is presented to Tad Sweaty of Happy Trailz.

"Holy shit," I said aloud. I was in the home of a boy-bander. Giddy with excitement I ran over to Frank and Chet who were sitting on a couch in front of a dirty mirror next to a cute blonde girl in a slightly oversized Vans shirt.

"Guys. You will never guess where we are."

"I bet I will. We are obviously in a huge pile of shit," Chet said.

"The guy who lives here was in Happy Trailz! The cornrow dude with the space goggles!"

"SHUT. UP," Chet yelled, sensing a story was in the making.

"For real. Come here. Look."

We traversed the room, giggling the entire way. I led him over to the record on the wall and he read the inscription aloud. Chet stopped laughing and became deathly serious.

"We have to find him. I need to get him high."

For half an hour Chet and Frank and I moved through the house with the intensity of a SWAT team. We opened doors hurriedly and waved each other in silently. In one of the bathrooms we found Cube who was standing near the toilet.

"Gentlemen. Come in. This wonderful young lady was going to show me how she can fit an entire bottle of beer in her asshole." I entered in disbelief, but sure enough, bent over the countertop, was a woman with her pants around her ankles. She had long black hair, gauges in her ears, and she was covered in tattoos so fully that she didn't strike me as being naked at all. Her left hand was on the mirror in front of her, and her right was slowly twisting a bottle into the depths of her own body. She looked up and my eyes caught hers in the reflection.

"Nice form." Her eyes rolled back into her head. She groaned.

"Motherfucker, you are in a mansion," Chet yelled at her. "Not in the porta-potty at a Metallica concert. Have some class. Use an imported beer." Chet walked over to her, pulled the Budweiser bottle out of her ass and handed her his half full Corona. "Ray. Let's move."

The house proved to be a maze. The front door of the palace that we entered through originally was essentially the back of the house, and once inside you could go up a total of six floors and onto a roof which overlooked the ocean. There were, I believe, a total of seven areas that could be considered *living rooms* if they hadn't been decorated like a college dorm or a horny single mom's basement. In one of them we found a display case which had in it over twenty music awards, as well as a wooden doll version of Tad that was used in one of his band's videos. Frank gasped.

"I need it," he said, his eyes wide. He was high as a kite.

"Stop it. You're not stealing from this guy." Ignoring me completely, Frank turned the unlocked latch on the glass case and gasped.

"Dude. No. No."

"Fuck you, Dad. I'm taking it."

"Frank! Don't." I shut the case, stepped over a sleeping cat, and walked toward the doorway on the opposite side of the room that lead me into a massive kitchen outlined with sterling silver appliances and chalkboard-painted walls. Dicks of various shapes and sizes and azimuths and inferences had been drawn everywhere and they were each ejaculating on things ranging from a disembodied pair of perfectly spherical breasts to, oddly enough, a chocolate fountain. In the middle of the room was a marble island with barstools set up around the perimeter, and on top of the island were a dozen empty pizza boxes and empty bottles of wine and beer and a rolled up dollar bill on top of a mirrored tray.

"This is what happens when you give white trash a little money," Chet called out from behind me as he opened the fridge.

"There's nothing in here but beer. It's exactly like my house, and I fucking disgust myself."

I thoughtlessly picked up and immediately put back down a dildo that was sitting on the stovetop, no doubt a part of a *hysterical* joke that took place between the hours of 4:00 and 7:00 a.m. when the coke was still plentiful. I walked over to the window above the sink and looked out over the water. A few stars flickered in the purple sky. I saw the headlights of a boat tracing the subtle waves, and faintly heard the music and laughter coming from four floors up that projected out over a glistening pool. It was a view I had always dreamed of having one day, but in pondering the conditions I longed to have in front of me, I failed to recognize the possibility that behind me would be crudely drawn dicks, drug residue, and a sex toy. There really was no point in having a vision that didn't revolve a full 360 degrees because it was usually from behind that life would sneak up and overtake you. Frank walked past, breaking my reverie with a slight brush of his book bag against my arm. He always had his bag on him. It held the cash from the show, and obviously he didn't trust leaving it in a van. I followed him down a hall that was adorned with more silver and gold and platinum records and enormous framed tour posters, and I grew more and more fascinated. Such prestige and wealth and fame and experience, and at the end of the day he lay his head *here*, in this museum of decadence? This wasn't a great like Jimmy Page or Mick Jagger or even a notorious animal like Nikki Sixx. This was Tad Sweaty. He danced with other guys onstage in front of thirteen-year-old girls, and with their money, he bought a chocolate fountain that he used only once. Then I heard the moaning.

"Is somebody fucking?" I whispered to Frank.

"Like, somewhere on earth?"

"No, here. Listen." Frank ducked his head for some reason, as if that would assist his hearing. Apparently, it did.

"Yes! People are absolutely fucking!" We crept down the hall. There was definitely a girl. Now there were definitely two girls. Now three.

"It's an orgy," Frank said matter-of-factly as we stood outside of a closed oak door. "This is gonna be like *Eyes Wide Shut*. A buncha sexy-ass rich people in masks and cloaks."

"Oh my god," Chet exclaimed. "What if it's an all boy-band ritual where the new members get sucked and fucked into the group? I'm going for it. I want to be famous. Wish me luck."

I held my breath as he bent low and opened the door slowly, but the process was sped up as more information of what lie behind it was revealed. In an instant, he was standing straight up in the frame of a wide open door that separated the hallway from a small movie theater with a look on his face comparable to the one you would see on the guy in a game show who gives up a *guaranteed* thousand dollars to gamble on a box that ends up having rotten fruit inside of it. I walked in behind him, my excitement decaying first into confusion and then disappointment and finally into a skin-crawling sense of embarrassment and depression. There was Tad, alone in his home theater, fully clothed, watching a pornographic movie.

"What up?" he shouted. "You motherfuckers lost?"

"Not at all," Chet said, unable to mask his enthusiasm for the things that were unfolding before him.

"Come in. Have a seat. Hope y'all dudes ain't gay because you definitely will not appreciate tonight's feature presentation."

Chet and Frank and I walked up to the back row, shook his hand and sat down just as girl number two pulled her fingers out of girl number one.

"Nice to meet you. I'm a huge fan," I said, though I was most certainly not a huge fan.

"You want some blow?" Chet asked, not the least bit cautiously.

"Naw, my mom might be home any minute. Hell, yes I want some blow."

"Frank, be a dear and hand me the illegal drugs." Frank enthusiastically opened his bag to retrieve Chet's coke, and as he did so a small wooden figure that resembled Tad fell out onto the floor. Tad looked down at it, processed the information, looked back up at us in disbelief, then stood up and spread his arms out like he was going to take flight.

"Yo."

Frank looked at him and back at me with his eyes wide and his lips pursed in front of a hidden, dropped jaw. Tad hopped over the rows of seats in front of him and began calling out for someone or something named Large, which I assumed to be a security guard of incredible magnitude. He failed to overcome the sounds of three exceptionally horny women on-screen, but it didn't stop him from trying.

"I fucking told you, Frank. Goddamn it."

Frank shoved the doll back into his bag, zipped it up, and followed as Chet and I rushed out into the hallway and down the spiral stairs through a crowd of people that were very much aware something in the house was amiss because they were silent. We found Cube at the bottom near the bar.

"Some fucking massive dudes just went up the back stairs looking for you," he said. "Do I have to get arrested tonight on assault charges?"

"Not if we leave like now. Frank totally blew it." We scurried out the door, fired up the van, and hastily retreated.

As I drove, Chet regaled Cube with every single detail of the night's impossibly odd events while Frank smiled on, proudly clutching his stolen doll. There was nothing he loved more than hearing stories about himself. It didn't matter to him in the slightest that it put the rest of us in harms way or that we may have wanted to stay and party a while longer. He was the center of attention and you could see it in his eyes that he was thrilled. Meanwhile, Chet's face lit up as he told them of the unlocked display case and their faces caught the same bright flame that spread joyously. Chet moved his hands as he spoke, like a conductor or a puppeteer, and indulged in every micro emotion as if he were back there once again in that room looking on as an observer to his own experience, both in and out of himself. He was traveling through time and we were his passengers. I could genuinely feel the disgust he felt when looking through the fridge and the disbelief in his heart when he saw the man-boy, who owned the ten-million-dollar home, watching porn alone on a thirty-foot screen. His stories had the ability to transport anyone listening to the exact moment of creation as if his words didn't stand for something real, but were something real in themselves and, as a writer—which I *was*, despite what that sanctimonious asshole roommate of mine had told me— it was a talent I sought but could for now only breathlessly admire in a true adept like Chet. Through him, there was no awe lost in the translation from being told. His stories were not paintings of a glory that he had witnessed; they were a guided path that we walked to witness it for ourselves. He was a perfect medium for the unspeakable beauty of our fantastically dysfunctional lives, designing while we observed genesis.

Hundreds of miles away, Claire was packing her bags. When I returned home two weeks later, she was gone.

CHAPTER TWENTY-FIVE

I AWOKE DRENCHED IN SUN ON A RED RUG in the middle of the floor of a filthy room. Billions of dust particles glimmered madly around me, filling the musty air and blanketing every fixture, every habit, every action, and every word like old sheets draped over gaudy heirlooms. Old clocks. Antiquated electronics. An unfinished marble statue of a boy with grotesquely unnatural features loomed next to a pile of damp books. Hulking muscles tacked onto frail bones and loose skin dripping off the frame evidenced the artist's unfamiliarity with form and space. Fungus gathered on a pile of gold bricks. I didn't recognize the room, but my dream self felt a sense of ownership over its contents, over all these certainties that had been stockpiled and were now decaying as a plant might when taken out of fertile soil. I was disgusted at the condition of these things—*my* things— but only now was light coming into the room. They and I had been in darkness for so long. How could I have known? The needle of a record player jumped to the same spot on a warped piece of vinyl, incessantly churning out the same phrase until it was etched into the atmosphere in the same way a carving tool in the right hands digs masterfully through a block of dried wood or a stream of water might run through stone.

Welcome to Mind Magic. You are worthy of your life.

The mantra echoed bewitchingly, and under it even the immovable nothingness itself sat quietly yawning and collecting dust. I didn't recognize a thing from where I stood, but the brilliance of the sun illuminated the filth that surrounded me like the morning light creeping into an all-night drinking binge through living room blinds. But more than that, more than just reliably vanquishing darkness as the sun always had, it called my awareness to all it touched, a dawning that was sad and sublime and crippling and full. In that room where time had suffocated all, my dreams were bloated with death and not a thing was true. Who was I in here? These were the gears that drove me on? This was my center of operations? Pitiful. Not moons that moved a powerful tide, these belongings were softly humming bulbs that distracted a thoughtless insect. I felt humiliated by the cluelessness of man. Had anyone loved me, they had been fools. Only those who sought it and failed deserved it at all. I thought of Hannah, existing somewhere beyond that room in the realm of unmitigated magnificence who would venture from it into any slum with unshaken faith that she could draw me out. But I, surrounded by myth, never showed. She knocked and I refused her an answer. Because I was ashamed? Yes, that was it. Shame. I sensed what was in the darkness of my room and I sensed it was ill, but without light, things can be as large as uncertainty will allow. I postured to protect my weak young from those that would laugh and pass judgment.

As that truth settled in, I began to sense that I was not alone. There was a fiend in there with me, something very much alive and heavy and almost reptilian in its uncompromising need for sustenance. Then, from the only corner light couldn't reach, came the low growl of an old dog. My pride. Companion and protector. As if responding to my humiliation, it emerged, hungrier than ever, its eyes black with hell. It gazed at me with a noble indifference before glancing toward the door as if we were expecting unwelcomed visitors. When none came, he returned his eyes to mine and something seemed to dawn on him. He lowered his head and stepped backward, gnashing his teeth as the fur on the back of its neck stood up. For the first time, here on the brink of a deep chasm, I understood the animal immediately and entirely without doubt. In the light of awareness, it saw its own death take my form. Effortlessly adapting to shifting concepts and landscapes that intuit the sense of having always been as only your dream self can, and my new but eternal purpose had no other option but to be fulfilled. In a past moment, I may have adopted beasts, but in this moment, I would slay them. It was all there was and could be nothing else. Then I was summoned back to the waking life that waited for me above.

"It's going to get cold," Evan said. "Come inside and crash on the couch." Another new landscape was suddenly before me, replacing the antiques of that battlefield I had just stood firmly upon. I knew this one, too, for I had also always been right there. I stood up and followed Evan inside, moving trustfully but clumsily atop the blurry world.

CHAPTER TWENTY-SIX

CLAIRE HAUNTED ME FOR THE ENTIRETY OF the long drive home, her still-vivid form delighting in the golden beams of attentiveness for the first time since I abruptly locked her between the pages of an endless story. Once out of the shadows of the compounded transgressions I stacked in front of her, her memory revealed itself as something too gentle to master the strategies of battle that my life required her to reconcile. Her delicate weaponry stood no chance against the giants of lust and loathing that I had been partnered with. I found myself wishing now that I could have sided with her. I wanted to know how to cherish her for handling my clumsy heart instead of daring her to take it from me as I so often had, but shielding it in secrecy was the only way I could convince anyone there was any value to it at all, because my truth was that the source of the echo that amplified through it had been quiet for years.

Once I had begun touring full time, almost my entire relationship with Claire was spent in the abject nothingness of other's far-less-moderate hands and because of this, I learned quickly that there was a hell you needn't wait for death to deliver. It was in every moment that slunk in the wake of falseness and it wasn't rife with gnashing flames or soaked in deep groans but devoid of all, grey and cold and silent. The hell I found in the guilt I felt had no one to confess to, no relief from the strain that the innocence of just being puts rightfully on your shoulders and you cannot roll away with reason the heavy terribleness that your deceitful lust has borne or all the selfish ways you irreversibly wounded everything in creation, no matter how hard you push your thoughts against them to make room to breathe deep. In that hell, time has whisked away all deeds to distant corners and leaves you standing there, lost in a desert of ice hoping with all your might that you will wake from despair like a bad dream and beauty will surround you or, as I chose to do in the days and weeks and months following every ghastly reoccurrence when I found this wish of sleep to be itself a dream, you lie and you drink until grand concepts like reality are diluted in a storm of murky poison. You tell yourself that what actually happened back in that hotel room hadn't actually happened in that hotel room or that stability cannot be expected when your fate is on a fault line or that you are a lonely man with a poet's heart who has no option but to behave as pitifully as your muse demands or that you just needed to feel something after so much nothingness and your weakness is an involuntary response to a cruel god that you don't even believe exists. Anything to construct a new safe place where the melancholic freeze can't find you. But all this is done to the detriment of your mind which is so tired from spinning the plates of so many different weights and sizes that it threatens collapse like a universe out of momentum, so you postpone decay by putting the inarguable tenet that it really truly did happen far in the back of your heart where it rots and takes up room that love could be occupying knowing one day it will just be all hard and black like an old rose, and because it is full of such incomprehensible truths, you believe, but will never say, that one day soon it will not serve you in the ways it was meant to serve you. It will pump blood and it will skip occasionally but that doesn't even matter since it will not love another person well, no matter how hard you beg it to love another person well, and like a car that won't start, it sits there hopelessly gasping and you know that it is your fault that it can't be moved, so you drink even more because awareness of a lost way is the worst thing a creature on this earth can possibly have and when you lose sight of beauty you gain ownership of all the knowledge of everything evil that has ever been. You wish only to drown deeper because the acute agony felt in every nerve as you sink into your bottle is a welcomed distraction from the certainty of the pain your lust has howled into the garden. You stand alone in hell looking only into the dead eyes of your grim past. You are so sad and feel so disconnected from joy and love itself that when someone—anyone at all—reaches out to you in the mist that holds you back from the goodness of life like an unbreachable ravine you will become so thankful for her touch that reminds you of the girl you were sent to protect that you will kiss her lips and make yourself believe that interruption from grief might be what love is now but it is not, it is just another cruel trick hell plays on its slaves. It was only more wretchedness, because what even an absent god knows is that love is unmistakable. Love is unmistakable and nobody loves you like the one who waits. Claire, whose eyes were life-giving, was unimpressed by your music because she makes her own even in silence but drink makes you forget that and so another body goes on the pile on the mattress and more pitch black gets stuffed into you only to be amplified back into the world as it beats oblivion like a drum and starving, ravenous hell becomes colder because foolish nihility has tied itself to every word you sing and soon everyone who hears your pitiful voice has unwittingly welcomed it into their own heart like the cold blue flame of a candle spreading sick light, and when they internalize it and sing it back to you out loud, they too have caught the frost and the devil is shaken to the surface and so cycles the plague of despair. If it happens once, it happens for the rest of your life. When the devil is allowed into your consciousness it understands that there it belongs and you wear the mark forever. Your life wears the mark forever.

But does your death? There were moments where I had thought of finding out for sure. So deep was my need to escape that nagging woe that if handed a blade I knew I would not hesitate one second to take the long risk just because there might be a chance that I would wake up and see goodness smiling over me like Claire used to. There still were those times.

What happens on the road takes that same road home and is alongside of you no matter what speed you travel. You can never outrun it. And in that home you are so afraid of every eternal moment of every otherwise perfect day because you fear your vile specters will call out to you and reveal themselves from inside your own shadow and so you cannot think about doing the things that a good person should do for the people who love them. You cannot resign to the vibrations of their voice because you are coiled up tight, trembling, wincing, waiting in fear of a "something" approaching that will not make known what direction it is approaching from until it is upon you, but sometimes you can hear it teasing you from a dark sea and when you do, you weep because you are so unfathomably frightened of watching it destroy what it stalks. And when that someone who loves you asks you why you're weeping, you cannot tell them that it's because a little bit of hell has come back for you because no one who is lovely like Claire was will ever understand what you mean by sorrow and you cannot explain because hell is where no one shares a thing. Not even language. Then, when those devils retreat, their bellies full of the sleep they have stolen, all you can say is "I'm sorry," but the saying is empty because nothing you say can ever fix the dent your selfishness made in the purity that drifts above words, and when a person who loves you as Claire loved me asks what you are sorry for you cannot ever ever ever tell them because it would cloud their path with fear and they would love you no longer, and only when loveless can one enter that sad chasm. If they knew what you had done to them, if they knew how you had denied them, forgotten them, buried them, they could not ever love like they once did and the cruelest thing you can do to someone is to share the rot and rob them of the glorious mystery of being in love because faith in it is really all anyone ever has to know. I pushed Claire away because I had been down too long and she was too divine to know that anything but perfection was destined to be hers.

Meanwhile, the poor, poor world passed by outside the van, still beautiful and blissfully unaware of how much dread had been tucked into the hearts of those it cherished most.

CHAPTER TWENTY-SEVEN

AT NINE O'CLOCK THE NEXT MORNING, Evan drove me back to the bus where our goodbye was brief and precise.

"I'm glad you got in touch with me. I don't know why you did, but I think we're both better for it."

"Honestly, I came for the apology I felt I was owed. Now I feel like I should be the one apologizing to you."

"No need," Evan said. "Water under the bridge."

"I'll call you next time I'm out this way." Evan smiled but said nothing. Then he got in his jeep and left.

Inside the bus, Chet was asleep on the couch of the front lounge, sitting fully upright next to the table as if his cord had been pulled out of the wall in mid sentence. In front of him was an empty fifth of vodka, a dozen beer cans and a rolled up hundred-dollar bill. Cube came out of the back holding his laptop.

"Holy shit. Looks like I missed quite an event! 'The Slow Death of Your Friend' sponsored by Jagermeister and cocaine. All of the biggest fucking losers were in attendance." Chet powered up again and moaned. "And where did you speed off to?" Cube asked at me. "Too cool to hang out with your pals?"

"I went to an old friend's house. Remember Evan? He used to live with me and Frank. He came to your bar with us sometimes."

"Oh yes", Cube said, removing his glasses and cleaning the lenses with his T-shirt. "Wonderful little gay man."

"What? No. You think he's gay? Is he gay?"

"I definitely got that vibe." he said as he put his glasses back on. "Either way, you missed a LOT of hot action, let me tell you. Your friend Chet here", Cube poked Chet's temple with his index finger, "inhaled a glacier of dude and almost chewed his tongue off while playing Oasis songs for about ten hours straight." He laughed. "And then he just fucking left. Said he had to go see a man about a horse. I seriously can't believe he made it back here. Hey Chet." Cube yelled as he kicked the seat. Chet shifted his pale body. "Chet. You got everything you need? You didn't leave your phone at a rave in an abandoned coal mine or something insane like that did you? We gotta get moving. Dallas ain't close".

"I'll get a new one tomorrow." Chet groaned, pressing his head against the window and going back to sleep.

By chance, Alkaline Trio had a day off in Dallas on the night of my show. I had all of them put on the guest list but only a few guys were actually dumb enough to spend a rare day off inside a music venue. When I returned to the dressing room from the stage after my set, it was bustling with drunk company. Matt was locked in a deep conversation on the couch behind a pile of cigarette butts with our mutual friend Jorma who played drums for The Bronx, a band I used to tour with when my career first started. Matt was wearing a thick line of mascara underneath each of his eyes, which only intensified his gaze. His exuberance and flamboyant body language reminded me of a lot of Chet's, but Matt was given the artistic license that Chet was not so it didn't seem so much "batshit crazy" as it did "persona-enhancing", though truthfully there was no difference between his on and off stage personalities. Jorma was just smiling and shaking his head, no doubt being told something bordering on psychotic.

"Ray!" Matt yelled, catching me in his periphery. His eyes were as wild as the first time we met. "That was FUCKING incredible!" He stood up and hugged me and handed me a beer.

"You liar. You have been sitting back here all night," I said, twisting off the top.

"Yes, yes I have, ok? I wanted to watch you but I didn't. But that doesn't mean it wasn't fucking incredible. I have seen you before. I know what you do. Was it fun? Was it good?"

"Meh," I replied, shrugging. "It was alright." But something about it felt different. Unfulfilling. I couldn't really put my finger on it.

"We all have those nights. Packed house, though."

"Yeah." I said, reassuring myself. "Sold out. Tour is going well."

Jorma stepped out from behind the couch and hugged me. "Come here buddy. What a nice surprise." I said. "Such a wild coincidence. I didn't even know you guys were on tour until Cube saw it online this morning."

"No coincidences, brother." Matt took a pull off a bottle of whiskey. "So listen to this. I was just telling Jorma about how I met David fucking Lynch at a restaurant a little while ago and how he's actually becoming somewhat of my guru. Like, a personal spiritual advisor."

"It's a real shame I'll never find out how this story ends." Jorma said sarcastically as he turned quickly and left the room altogether.

"Whatever. His loss. So yeah. Dude. It's called Transcendental Meditation. You ever hear of it? I'm on that wave now. I mean I AM that wave now. You gotta fucking get into it man. It's perfect for you. It's perfect for the whole world but they're not all ready for it. You first. Well, David first and then me first and then you first. But that's how it goes. Like a flame. Like from me to you." Matt was on overdrive. "David has a school. And I met him at some art exhibit in this fucking sleazy-ass LA warehouse and we talked forever and now he's like actually overseeing my spiritual training. He wants me to be his student. I'm just teething right now. I'm in the teething phase. Very uncomfortable and weird. But it's evolution. Intelligence evolution. He's giving me his light and now I have it to give to someone else. But see that's how, like, light works, you know? When you put a candle up to another candle it doesn't like, go out from the original candle after the flame is transferred, right? It just gives its light and they both glow on! So even if I bring this light to you, I still have it too and now we both glow together, you get it? And that happens no matter how many candles you touch, until the whole world is illuminated! It's fucking beautiful!"

"Matt. Calm down. I just got done playing. Can I shower first? Christ."

"Okay, but then I'm going to turn you on. You promise to let me? You promise to let me turn you on to this? Don't just fucking say it to shut me up Ray, don't you fucking do it." I said nothing as I closed the bathroom door behind me.

I stood in the shower for an inconsiderate amount of time, stalling, trying to ignore and distract myself from what Matt had said and the subtle ways in which it reminded me of my conversation with Evan just one night before. Meditation had always seemed like a fad diet to me. I had forever equated it with new age hippie bullshit, which was just a pastime of lazy burnouts the way football was the pastime of horny jocks. Sure my mother did it occasionally, but she was an old woman who loved to garden. What could it offer me that drinking couldn't? Weren't they both about fleeing from yourself? Meditating was not something people "like me" did; people who thrived on discord and unrest. A poet had no use for peace.

But who are people like you? I heard Dr. Singer asking. *What are their characteristics?* Were they confused or were they self-assured? Because I was both. Were they surrounded by friends or were they

lonely all the time? Because I certainly was both. Were they slaves
to human impulse, or were they masters of a craft? Would they rip
a classmate's shirt off his back, or pay to put one on? Were they
lustful, or in love? It was exactly the type of thing Evan and I had
just spoken about, not to mention the fact that since only yesterday
the space that my life occupied began to bend just slightly around a
vague concept of "god" in the way that water circles a drain. While
what "is" remains unseen, the behavior of things around it indicate
that they are indeed in the presence of something all-consuming.
I could not see it if I stared directly at it, nor could I approach it
with any hopes of returning to the spot where I stood before I set
out to reach it, but it was there. I couldn't articulate it, but I felt it.
I dried off, clothed myself, and stepped out of the bathroom into
a dressing room now even more full of faces, some I recognized,
some I didn't. Matt was standing next to Chet who was cutting up a
line of cocaine on the countertop. Jorma was laughing manically as
he drunkenly chatted with a beautiful girl who had a rose tattooed
on the side of her neck.

"So you want to talk somewhere?" I asked Matt, hesitantly.

"Ray, yes I absolutely do I absolutely do want to talk to you but
I have to finish my drink and then I have to try to fuck that girl" he
said, pointing to a tall, skinny girl with a buzz cut standing alone
near the fridge, who saw him point and eagerly waved back.

"Are you allowed to walk the path toward enlightenment with
a hard on?"

"Enlightenment isn't a place at the end of a path, dude. It's the
entire shore on the other side of an ocean. And, yes. You can have
a boner. You come as you are."

"Well, good luck with that girl. She loves being choked and I
don't know if this gentle new you will be able to please."

"No, no, no, wait" he said, reaching into a handbag he had
draped over his shoulder. "Take this book. Don't worry about giving

it back. But when you're done, you have to give it to someone else. You have to light another candle." He handed me a thick yellow book with a drawing of an old bearded Indian man on the cover. "This is your bible now." he said earnestly. "Except there are no rules or instructions or scores to be kept. It's just suggestions. If you want to change your life, then abide them. And if you don't? It's not for you. No threats of hell or anything like that. " I looked the book over front and back and rifled through the pages. I thought it had a surprising heft to it, considering meditation was little more than "sit still and be quiet."

"Thanks. Actually," I said rather proudly, "I've been doing a lot of self-hypnosis so this could definitely help." Matt looked at me like I had handed him a crying baby.

"You're doing what? Raymond. No." He turned his back to Chet, finally giving me his full attention.

"Good, more dude for me!" Chet said, quickly inhaling two thick lines of white powder which he cordially referred to as "the dude." Matt ignored him entirely.

"That is nothing like this. How long have you been doing it? How far back have you been set?" I was confused.

"Just a few weeks now. I don't get it. Why's it a setback?"

"Okay, let me guess. You paid a bunch of money to some shrink and now you got a weird little voice floating around in your headphones telling you that you're awesome."

"Well, okay, I mean yeah, exactly that. It's called Mind Magic. It uses subconscious messages to change the way you think about yourself while you sleep."

"Oh, that's great," he said sarcastically, shrugging. "So even when you're asleep your ego gets a workout. The ego is the root of every single problem in the history of man. This book," he said, tapping his finger down on it as it rested in my hand, "Will prove that to you. You're not what your brain tells you you are," he went on. "Those little voices are lying. Truth isn't spoken. It just is."

I grew defensive. "Matt you're wearing makeup."

"Hey man, that's expression. That's freedom, brother. And when I apply my makeup, I do so from a place of truth. I do it because I want to. Because it's natural and it works for me. You'll realize that you are a very small part of a very great whole that can still allow you such marvelous opportunities. And while that may make you feel powerless, it's actually a beautiful thing to know. Like you're a little worker bee personally chosen to build a galaxy-sized hive. A cell working fastidiously in the body of god."

"That sounds like a textbook cult mentality. " I said, getting increasingly irritated at his flagrant dismissal of my hypnotherapy.

"So what. This punch is refreshing."

CHAPTER TWENTY-EIGHT

EDDIE'S FATHER DIED OF PANCREATIC CANCER in the fall of 2005, not long after I had last spoken to him. With Claire and I separated, I found myself longing for the comforts of timeworn habits, those that preceded my top-heavy lunge into the music world. Rekindling a friendship with Eddie seemed like the natural step backward onto familiar shores. Since Evan and I had never fully recovered what we lost after his unsolicited "intervention" about my writing, he offered to move out in the wake of Claire's departure, and I was happy to see him go.

Unable and unwilling to find a mutual friend that could fill his space, Frank and I also agreed to go our own ways, though on much better terms. We were both making enough money touring to afford small places of our own and with us now working together so closely on the road, it was best to have some room in-between tours and not put our careers at risk under the weight of auxiliary tensions sprung from a domestic dispute. I moved into a one-bedroom apartment on the third floor of a renovated office building in the heart of Ithaca's "art district," and he stayed further uptown by the campus where the young meat of the college girls that knew him from online was more tender. With all sameness freed, our personal demons plunged excitedly into the feast.

Having lost the love of Claire, the friendship of Evan, and the constant presence of Frank all within a few months, made my time spent with Eddie that much more valuable. He helped me feel more grounded, like I was holding the hand of someone stationed permanently on the steady terrain of the past while I dipped my toes into choppy waters. It was a commitment to noncommitment, a playing of all roles in order to insure that I never fully lost myself in any one thing. This way, I figured, I could maintain control over which compartments my life was put into rather than allowing it to run off with the entirety of me. It didn't matter that Eddie was not the mentor I had once desperately sought, he was the only string that connected my kite to the earth.

On a Friday night during the summer before his father's death, Eddie and I were in my apartment drinking and he was again rancorously arguing that 9/11 was an inside job. I had heard all of his theories before but I staunchly refused to believe them, so preposterous to me was the idea that the people we trusted would ever harm us or that total chaos wasn't the gold standard of life on earth.

"Your truth is wrong." I remember him saying, as if that platitude made any sense to anyone. "Whatever you knew about America or whatever it was to your grandfather? It isn't that anymore. Our own government did this in order to have a reason to go to war, and they did it right in front of us because we are too dumb and too lazy to do anything about it and they fucking know it. They are counting on good Americans like you to trust them because you're still so confused about what happened on that day. And just because you don't see it, doesn't mean it hasn't always been there."

As was par for the course after our first dozen beers, the window of him being the funniest, smartest, most awe-full guy I knew had shut tight, and at around midnight he had officially staggered into the stage of his intoxication where he would rub his hands together compulsively as if washing them clean of an invisible filth. It was with this phase shift that he began nervously approaching the subject of his dad, using half sentences and thrusting nonverbal communicators toward me when the words could not be retrieved from the cloud of alcohol that set in over his third eye.

"See the thing is?" he said, sadly. "My dad just, I mean... hmmmm." His eyes became shiny. "Okay, you know, it's just..." He leaned forward, either inching toward or away from a darkness only he could recognize. The source of confusion was very obviously the looming death of his father. Soon Mr. Reilly would exist where words don't and to grasp even a part of that inconceivable truth meant that Eddie too was trapped in an adjective-less landscape, desperately trying to find the colors to paint a picture of a place that had never been seen, one that shunned description. It was a task as impossible as trying to convey the exact sense of nostalgia brought on by a certain smell because death circumvented all logical connections to our world and deftly eluded prose. The place where Eddies father dying actually made sense to Eddie was located in a valley that no one else's brain had, and it became so personal that it partnered with first love. I could, however, understand that such valleys existed, so the least I could do for him that night was to stand at the brink of where my truth ended and his began and listen for him to call out from inside of it in desperate wails. I could only bear witness, understanding that though I may not be able to make out the words, the very presence of a voice meant that Eddie was still there and trying to make sense of the terrible mess he was in.

"I have to call him," he said. "I think he'd like your take on all of it."

"My take on death? I don't have one," I said nonchalantly, ashing my cigarette into the small opening of an empty beer bottle in front of me.

"I know that. I know that. Okay. I know that." His hands were twisting in and out of each other like two eagles mating in midair. "But maybe that's what he should hear. Maybe he needs you to remind him that life is shit. If death is the only certainty… and and and and meaning, then…"

My typically unflinching fatalism recoiled in the presence of Eddie's gigantic and sad inevitability. Hopelessness should be reserved for the living. Let the dying keep their faith.

"No, I don't think he needs to hear that. I think he needs distraction." But Eddie was already dialing. It didn't matter that it was late. The importance of what time it is probably vanishes pretty quickly when you realize that you don't have much left. Eddie handed the phone over to me.

I knew that this conversation Eddie forced upon me was more of way to bide time, just something in that specific family's gene pool that drove Eddie and his father and probably drove his grandfather and will one day drive Eddie's son to interact with another person on any level at all before life is done sharing itself with them and there was an insincerity to it that I sometimes resented. Eddie was a collector. He visited, gathered, hoarded, used, and referenced, but these things didn't quite equate to connecting. Sometimes when I watched Eddie listen to people, I knew that he wasn't doing it to understand, he was doing it because it was mandatory before responding. For that reason, I was guarded when handed the phone. I didn't want to risk having my pessimism dismantled, but I had also never spoken to someone very literally on their death bed. I reluctantly took the phone.

"Hello, sir. I'm sorry Eddie called you so late, I tried to stop him."

"He's an inconsiderate garbage bag full of shit when he drinks. I'm used to it."

"So, how are you feeling?"

"Like hell, how do you think?"

"If hell existed, I'd imagine just like it."

"I was in Vietnam. I can assure you it exists."

"Okay, but war and suffering and loss and all the stuff associated with war, that's only metaphorically hell. You're not afraid of an actual place called Hell, are you? Capital 'H.' Like, a literal geographical location where your soul goes?"

"My soul came here to war, didn't it? What's the difference?"

"Well, I'm not going to argue with you that life is mostly shit, but I refuse to believe that our souls are going anywhere particular after this."

"That's because you're too stupid to notice anything you've lost coming back to you as something else."

"Well I think it's stupid to believe in reincarnation just because you're scared to be nothing when you die."

"Here's the thing about me dying, Ray. I get to believe everything I want. And it's not because I'm scared, you spoiled little shit. It's because facing death makes me see that nothing is more real than anything else. While the war was happening, I knew it would one day be over. But I also knew that it would never end. Have you ever been certain of two opposite things at the same time?"

"It's not possible. There's no way The Vietnam War could have lasted *forever*."

"That's not the war I'm talking about." He coughed. "Put my asshole son back on the phone. And be safe on the road please. Eddie is going to need your help real soon." I handed it over to Eddie.

He may have thought me to be foolish, but I was at least resolute. I had stuck to the script, ideologies as consistent as ever. My nihilism was still firmly dug in, even in the face of the most formidable enemy, though when he passed a few weeks later, a part of me secretly hoped he was somewhere enjoying how wrong I had been.

At the funeral Eddie seemed to be admirably okay with death, almost as if the detection of cancer a year prior was the real finale and the time in-between then and now was granted to him in order that he might practice dealing with it before the physical representation of his father was removed from sight forever. By the time they put him in the ground, Eddie had fully understood that it was just the next symbol in a formula, and he didn't shed a tear.

After the service, inside of what was now his widowed mother's home, Eddie handed me a flask that he pulled out of the pocket of his corduroy blazer. I took a sip of the warm whiskey inside of it and made no pretension of it being any good.

"Yeah. This shit sucks, but it was his favorite. This is his flask. Booze was still in it." He took another sip. "Pretty solid turnout, huh? LOTS of trim." It was then that I saw her, standing in the corner of the living room, talking to Eddie's mother.

"Fuck is Hannah doing here?"

"Her family lived down the street when we were little. My parents used to babysit her. We even dated for a little bit. I probably could have fucked her if you hadn't blown it for me.

"In seventh grade?"

"Absolutely. I already had a ton of pubes. Chicks would have loved it."

Where we had grown up, seventh and eighth grade were in their own building fifteen minutes by bus from my home. It was like a brief period of limbo as you transitioned from the childishness of elementary school to the horny teenage awkwardness of high school. Whereas grades one through six consisted only of other children that lived in your neighborhood, seventh grade was the first time you would ever come across kids from other suburbs, so those two years were spent floating around, bumping aimlessly into other particles after you had gained a consciousness, but before you began to actually take shape.

On the very first day, us new students were summoned from our homerooms over the PA systems by a stern, bodiless man and told to head toward the auditorium where we would be briefed on things like class schedules, the buildings layout, and locker combinations; in other words, where we would be introduced to the three components of every single one of our eventual adult nightmares. There was absolutely no order to the gathering that morning, save an elderly biology teacher named Mrs. Z who would occasionally stop the march she was leading down vast sterile hallways to turn around and "shhhuush" us when we became too riled up. Not a single one of my friends from the neighborhood was in that first class with me, so when I took a seat in the auditorium that we eventually filed into, I did so only because a boy who I happened to be walking next to sat down first. As soon as I settled in, the girl in front of me turned around, her long blonde hair swooping dramatically over her shoulder.

"Hi, what is your name?" she asked robotically.

"Raymond."

"Hi Raymond, my name is Rachel and this is my best friend Hannah." Next to Rachel, as if waiting years for her cue, the body of a girl with a head of straight brown hair sunk down a few inches and then very carefully turned herself around to present a gift of immeasurable value, little fingers gripping the top of the red plastic seat back as if holding a veil over the bottom half of her face. Everything else in the world completely disappeared. There was only the present, and it was always there in her eyes. In my life, I would never again love anything as much as I loved Hannah at that moment, and it would be years until I was again so immediately certain of purpose.

I began to call Hannah my girlfriend because it was the word I knew adults would expect children like us to use, though in every roar of delight that still occupied my bright young soul I heard something that surpassed any familiar experience, a feeling that came from a place far beyond the terrain where our senses might venture to hunt sustenance. She became the first piece of evidence that I was not just alive, but able to be loved, and the confidence that gave me urged me up many a great mountain, for when you are first loved you can assert yourself upon the world and make irrational demands of fate. Hannah and I guided each other into the thicket of adolescence but there was no word or symbol we could borrow from our home to take with us for safety. Nothing would translate into the language of the aging beasts that populated the adult realm. Were we just too immature to know one? If that was the case, when we were old enough to learn of it, would we be too old to remember what it was we wanted to describe when we felt it so concisely? At twelve years old I had seen our lives together as clearly as if a grand fisherman had pulled in his infinitely large net from all deltas and brought their contents back upstream to lay in front of me—a collection of innumerable futures returning to their source in a face that only halfway hovered above the back of an auditorium seat.

From that day on Hannah and I loved each other faithfully for years, but with an experienced fierceness that our inexperienced vessels almost couldn't handle. Something sublime was loaded into our frail containers and we were so overwhelmed by the great burden of knowing our other selves at such a tender age that had we not found the pressure valve of punk rock music when we did, we would have hemorrhaged. Bringing her that cassette tape from my trip downtown with Eddie was a fire theft and ignited in our Siamese minds the inextinguishable torch of resolve. Once its hooks were in us, we moved where it willed. We skipped classes in order to smoke cigarettes and listen to dubbed tapes with older skateboarders in the woods behind the school, we wrote each other solemn love poems and gave each other small tattoos with India ink and thread-wrapped needles at parties in abandoned houses, we grew our hair, ripped our jeans, lied to our parents on the weekends in order to drink in the woods, and when we lost our virginity to each other, it was in the bedroom of their home after I snuck her up the tree outside my window.

And yet, somehow, the burn dulled. Maybe it was that in the face of a fate that seemed almost administrative, my nerves sometimes longed for the rebellious experiences that they could use to refine themselves. Whatever it was—whether sincere or synthetic, whether felt or just heard—by the end of high school I began to feel that, despite our nonconformity, we were and always had been slaves to the stars that enticed us until one day, in the name of some vague punk rock crusade, I told Hannah I didn't love her anymore, and of all the lies I have ever told, that remains the most rotten. A few months later I was enrolled in a school far away, both stupefying providence and regaining full ownership of the life I was given.

But I had been Hannah's since the beginning of time and the world would have it no other way. So when I unexpectedly found her in Eddie's mothers house on the day of the funeral, I was speechless in the presence of a destiny that would not be denied even if postponed. Hannah and I had completely lost touch when I left for school. Maybe whatever it was that drove me to choose a college over her was strong enough to convince us both that we had been wrong about the future we simultaneously agreed on. Maybe we both lost faith and were too embarrassed to say anything. Maybe true love wasn't real. Either way, there she was, exactly where she needed to be. She had grown her hair out and allowed her natural brown to replace the pink I had last remembered it being. Her lips were fuller and lacked piercings, her clothes shorter and tighter, but her eyes were just as wide. She was no less beautiful than she had always been and she had unfolded according to the same schedule, all blooming things abide.

She must have sensed me looking at her, because she looked back. When her eyes met mine all wrong things receded. She pardoned herself and walked over.

"Hello, Raymond."

"Hi, Hannah"

"There are a lot of things I need to say to you." Her hands were shaking a bit, but her soft voice was confident.

"Me too."

"Not here. Let's talk outside." I lead the way into the backyard and she followed.

CHAPTER TWENTY-NINE

THE VENUE KICKED US OUT AT 1:00 A.M. Once we all said our drawn out and drunken goodbyes, I smoked a joint, took a few muscle relaxers, and stumbled onto the bus to finally return Hannah's phone call. She answered it groggily.

"Hey, it's me," I said, trying my hardest not to slur as the night air began to slither through my brain.

"Hi, baby. How was the show?"

"Meh. But Matt and Jorma were here. That was a nice surprise." Each word carefully mounted like a stepping stone up a sheer cliff.

"Uh oh. Look out. You guys get drunk?"

"No. I only had one small beer. How's the kid?"

Hannah laughed. "One small beer, huh?"

"Just one. Really small. How's Julius?"

"He's a fat little angel. We're watching TV on the couch."

"Don't let the dog on the couch, Hannah. He stinks."

"Come home and stop me. And don't talk about my little man that way. I raised him alone, you don't get to tell me I can't be nearer to him."

"Okay, I'm gonna go. You're ruining my vibe."

"Oh, I'm sorry Raymond. God forbid I ruin your buzz with stories of how I hold it down here so you can gallivant with little buddies."

"It's a job, like any other fucking job. I'm not just out here partying." I could feel an anger welling up, a need to defend myself against an enemy's indictment of my character. But Hannah, probably as a direct result of the soothing presence of our dog, returned to her center.

"Just please be safe. No talking to girls."

I pretended like I didn't hear the second part. "Yeah," I said, dismissively. You're being safe, too, right?"

"Yes, Raymond."

"You're not walking home alone anymore are you?"

"No, Raymond."

"If I find out you did, you'll be back in the hospital." I hostilely joked.

"That's not funny."

"Sorry. Just promise me."

She sighed. "I promise. I love you. Julius misses you."

"Love you, too."

"Say *I* love you, too, Raymond."

"I love you, too." Then she hung up the phone and I crawled into my bunk to quietly jerk off thinking of the girl in the dressing room who once begged me to choke her in the back seat of a car parked near a dark football field in New Jersey.

For the next two weeks of tour I tried rigorously to siphon a revelation from under Matt's new, exalted land but the wells I bore produced only friction. Unlike my Mind Magic tapes, the ideas that this "non-bible" posited were proofs written in a code I simply could not decipher with what little experience I had in holy things. These were mystic polemics that read like blueprints of a new wheel, metaphysical allegories that spoke of unfamiliar vistas from cosmic peaks to a musician toiling ceaselessly under fear of insignificance, a unity with the world underlying the division within himself, the illusory in the substantive, the particular in the universal, the effect in the cause, the God in the Man. But how could all that be? How could a temporary assemblage of faulty cells and mostly empty space invent the nightmares of the external world that befell him? Who would voluntarily summon such awfulness if it could be helped by something as simple as intention of will? How could I be the creator of my environment and a creation of it simultaneously? There was no logic to it. Multitudes were occupying the same spaces, flouting all maxims of exclusivity. My logical mind struggled desperately to grasp these ethereal notions, and though I could only find the answer to be moving further away the closer it advanced, I simply had no other choice but to study until I could understand. I needed to sift through the scraps of meat and the splinters of bone because the neon of all signs leading me to this spot were too bright to dismiss. Another bead of light was in there for me somewhere.

Perhaps maybe, to know truth, I would have to find it using something other than thought. I would have to, as Evan suggested, learn to let go of reason and submit entirely to a spirit that spoke without words. Not only was this counterintuitive, but for someone like me whose identity in the tangible world was based on the words I chose to represent the thoughts I had, relinquishing thought was a form of suicide. But hadn't I already familiarized myself with the location of that escape hatch? In the alcohol and the cocaine and the pills and the pot and the violence and the promiscuity, wasn't my hand already on the handle of the door, ready at any moment to throw it wide? If I could vanish and start over, couldn't I let a new destiny call on me rather than struggling to catch the attention of a god too preoccupied with those who worked hard to keep faith? What I actually needed was less than what I had, so what parts of me were worth keeping? If I were gone, if I were to give up my music, give up all my certainties, run away, change my name, take my own life, who would weep?

Hannah would be better off, that much was certain. All the compromises she made in her heart for my weaknesses of flesh, her years of patience for a love that only appeared in fits without warning and made no promises of return, entire seasons passing without passion, without a kiss, without a touch, abusive winds of rumor tearing the roof from our home and her quietly weathering it all without despair, surging waves of freezing doubt, her loyalty to a man that has never truly given himself to anything, her sincere promises made to the great oath-breaker, her gentle voice lost among the chorus of cackling ghouls, her shy, natural grandeur overshadowed by towering man-made amusements, her deep value questioned in the times when I allowed alcohol to usher me toward the aesthetic, all of those things would be vanquished with me and she could experience, for once, the glory of being Hannah. I had given too much to my fans to have anything left for her. They had my time and my attention and Hannah had a shotgun wedding instead of a beautiful ceremony and she trained a dog, though her soul longed to mother a child. She was supreme and deprived, and I was human and insatiable. In my death she would be relieved. In my life we would continue numbly on.

Eddie wouldn't give a fuck about me either. Just two days prior he had texted me saying that he was going drinking and I was welcome to join him. My oldest friend in the world had no idea that I hadn't been home in over a month. So while the invitation let me know that there was room for me in his company, it also assured me there was no need. Eddie had no desire for anything that I could possibly offer him. "Friend" was a role he played in my presence, never out of it. We held nothing valuable of each other's except the same fading images of the past. I was replaceable, just an audience at his performance. We would never make a plan or have a new idea because it was never our purpose to accompany each other upward. What good would it do my soul to scan the artifacts of our teen golden age even one more time? No good. I had to throw that reserve of tarnished silver to the bottom of the sea. Nothing about Eddie moved me anywhere but momentarily backward. He was the ghost of a primitive time that no longer existed for me. I could not press on if I voluntarily meandered down the dead ends. The progress I hoped to find with hypnosis would only come by dropping the weight of constant nostalgia. I never replied to his text and would not hear from him for months.

And what more did I owe my muse? How long could I continue carrying the light of a dead star through emptiness? I had grown too familiar with the science of songwriting to believe in the miracle of music anymore. It wasn't that I had ascended to the plane of my gods, it was that my music had the shameful ability to lure them into my depths where they could not hope to thrive. The atrocities that I would bear witness to ultimately dethroned everyone I once adored. I was granted access into a garden I once could only longingly gaze upon but I had paid a price to hold that key—the understanding that there were no gods in there at all. Instead, it was a town park littered with fallible bodies, burnt out on purity, unable to achieve salvation without trickery. Though something in me on a chemical level wanted a hero in the place where there were only monsters, the reality was that there never could be as long as the fire was out. And the fire was out.

So, what would be left for my fans? Nothing. Just as they deserved. Their period of mourning would be as disingenuous as their applause and last only until they were distracted by another similar explosion. At the speed of sound, every thing I built for them would decay, crumble and be forgotten and I would vanish unlamented. Our need for each other was not of the same source nor did it offer us the same spoils. I had regarded them always with suspicion and often with contempt. The ubiquity of camera phones and social media over the years made it difficult to trust people like I once had, impossible to simply let myself go. They had used me to show them the cold corners of their own lives and finding them too terrible to dwell in, they grew up, disavowed me, and continued onward. I, in turn, used them to give validity to my life on this earth as a lonely observer above the endless field of golden wheat, fixed permanently in the margins but gazing longingly into the center. Those that declared their "love" for me as they offered up poison, those who "respected" me as they gossiped of mutiny, "admired" me as they abused themselves. They didn't know a thing about me. And how could they? I wasn't here. I was outside of their gripes and pains and routines and worries. I knew nothing of the hungers of the common man. My clock was a different size than the ones that hung in their homes and offices; my only time, "stage time". My family was Chet and Cube and once there was Frank and they were assembled according to necessity, not genetics. My days were benchmarked by "soundcheck", "doors", "set," and "buscall," not alarms, lunch breaks, and bed.

When not present for those obligations I was a phantom, a black hole at the center of a swirling exhibition, containing nothing but consuming all. I drank too much and thought of death often. I escaped into the lives of others through the screen of my phone. I argued with my wife because it was the only time I felt passion anymore, I took downers with the secret hope of never waking up, I took uppers because I had been low for so long. I hurt deeply and without cause, I masturbated quickly and shamefully, I read books resentful of the fate that escaped me, my bones creaked, my muscled ached, my hair grew grey and my eyes sunk back into my head as if recoiling from the terror of everything I forced them to witness. I stood on stage in front of hundreds of people every single night to sing the same stories of grief, voluntarily putting myself back into the affairs and the fistfights, and the night that Hannah was mugged walking home while I was away on tour, conjuring up the helplessness amplified by the miles between us and the rage that flooded the world like a tide of animal fat pulled closer by an eclipse when I flew home and first saw her blue face in a white room.

I live in that hospital. Though she has recovered, I am stranded there. Every night in every city I build a new church to the disgrace that has imagined me, and though I move over the earth, I am transfixed under a moon which gives me light but no heat. And for what? So visitors could crowd around me and allow themselves to be briefly touched by my suffering before returning to the surface of the sphere that keeps them safe? That cares for them like they are its own young? To be reminded of the sadness they were lucky enough to have thwarted by fiercely and openly loving a strong woman whose hand they could confidently hold as she confessed her fear of her own illness instead of cowering under the cloak of night by a lake in the woods? The sadness I carried was rooted in my secrets, arm fulls of wet dirt held close to my chest. Oh, to be proud. To know what it felt like to not be sickened by the things I had done, to love someone enough to tell them what I really was—a thief. A vulture. A scoundrel. But who could love me then? Who would throw themselves into the grave that my love was? I was a mistress to an all-but-extinguished local haunt, a window in the asylum through which some peered into the chilling unknown and others saw only a grotesque reflection of their own tired visage. I was a horse broken early by a muse that abandoned me shortly thereafter. Bereft of purpose. A sled dog in the desert.

CHAPTER THIRTY

BY 2007 I WAS A CERTIFIED headlining act. I could sell out fifteen hundred–capacity rooms anywhere in the country. I had officially put Cube on the payroll as my Tour Manager and moved Frank to the position of Guitar Tech, which meant he worked less hours and received more pay while Chet was given a raise to be not only my sound engineer but my "Vibe Tech" as well—someone to keep me perpetually happy, drunk, and high. To the disappointment of our families, Hannah and I had gotten married on a whim when she came to visit me in Vegas, and when I returned home from that tour we eventually moved into a condo downtown and adopted a white bulldog. He already had the name Julius and we thought it sounded royal so we let him keep it. He became both our child and my emotional proxy for Hannah while I was away, soothing her by simply being. The minivan my mother bought for me was exchanged for an RV. I was, by all intents and purposes, a successful career musician. By 2008 I had played shows on four of seven continents, though my manager promised me that touring in the remaining three would be a reality if I wanted it to be. I had made a handful of music videos, and though MTV was no longer the force it once was in propelling a musician forward, online they had been viewed over a million times combined. This was considerably less than the number of hits Frank had received over all of his years as a YouTube celebrity, but the internet age was fickle, easily bored, and felt entitled to new stimulus, so as he watched his prominence steadily decline, he was forced to think of new ways to maintain relevance lest he disappear into the ether like an aged porn star whose saggy flesh could not possibly drum up desire.

The problem with my level of "stardom" was that it existed in a level below the awareness of the population. I was a slightly overweight man in my late twenties with zero marketability. I had a bloated face, I was stocky but lacked real tone, I was covered in faded tattoos, I smoked a lot of cigarettes, and I had exchanged my stifling need to be loved for a desire to be taken seriously as an artist. As camera phones became ubiquitous, I found that maintaining my privacy surpassed my hopes of being exposed and so while Frank gravitated hungrily toward attention, I awkwardly retreated. I had no mass appeal. I was not about to do photo shoots that required me to gaze lovingly into cameras holding my arms over my chest like someone at all afraid of real pain. I was going to play my guitar, smoke my throat into gravel, drink until it all stopped hurting, and flirt with the waitresses working the late shifts at middle-american diners.

This, however, was just as much of a character as any that could have been mocked up by any marketing team and so it brought with it a hyper-devoted fan base of like-minded men and women who, while smaller in number, were twice as rabid. Though I experienced no "real" celebrity in terms of hit singles on the radio or paparazzi fanfare, there was a subversive culture that put me on a ramshackle pedestal. I could walk unnoticed through swarms of teenage girls and their fathers but the second I went into a Guitar Center to buy strings, the one employee in the "Flaming Lips" T-shirt would act like Christ himself had walked there on water and incredulously ask everyone around him if they "knew who this was," which, of course, nobody did because they were real adults with jobs at Guitar Center.

Hannah found no amusement in it whatsoever. She was tired of me not making enough money to buy her plane tickets to visit me in cities overseas, but still having just enough distinction to get "fuck me eyes" from girls around town with hand tattoos. Hannah had no visible tattoos. Hannah didn't care much for my music either, as she preferred songs that made her happy to be alive rather than wish she wasn't. Hannah had fallen in love with Raymond when we were kids but quickly grew resentful of Ray in our adulthood, and I in turn became frustrated at her inability to keep up with the speed my life was traveling. We argued often and fucked infrequently.

When I did return home from tour, the transition from the road to an acceptable stasis would take about a week. I would find debts piled high, drinks that cost money out of my own pocket, and a woman who expected niceties and affection from the vagrant she had been faithfully waiting for. This seems easy enough of a concept to understand, except that I had just had so many women throwing themselves at me so frequently that I tended to forget the need for and importance of romance between two people who actually loved each other, so while I liked many people well, I found I loved not one person great.

Initially the shift is overwhelming. The walk through your own front door on the morning you arrive home is akin to passing through the threshold between dream and waking life, though much slower and more obvious. A world that only you experienced has completely and suddenly dissipated, and though it seemed real just moments ago, no remainders are allowed to exist in the daily hometown routine. Its rules simply do not apply there, the conditions will not sustain tour life. The magnitude of your conquests, your discomfort, your sacrifices none of them were lived in a language that is spoken off the road and attempting to convey any of it is as nonsensical as sleep talk.

In particular, the return from my first Warped Tour in 2009 felt even less remarkable than all other times, though exactly why I could not know. Perhaps I had woken out of the wrong dream, or woken into someone else's life. Either way it felt familiar but unnatural, like being in an empty high school classroom at midnight. I was uncertain of where to rest. Hannah was more agitated than ever, refusing to even come in off the balcony and greet me when I entered our apartment. She just stared off into space and seemed to be harboring a secret. Did she know what had happened that summer, of Sophia? No, she could not, but did she sense it? Did she need worldly proof to speak on otherworldly premonitions?

Meeting Sophia was a glitch in providence, so our relationship— or whatever it could be called for those two months of summer— avoided categorization like it had some nebulous gem hovering above it bending all revealing light and judgmental gazes away in order that our old souls could timidly meet in darkness and play like they belonged to curious teenagers rather than beaten-up musicians. She was a singer who grew up in Chicago but lived in LA and for ten years. She wrote all of her own music, funded all of her own recordings and fought all of her own wars, which meant that like me, she had been demoralized, she had felt embarrassed, she had acted shamefully, she had suffered stoically, and she had known grief well. But having emerged victorious, she was cynically hard-hearted and possessive of a thoroughly informed distrust of other people which I found peculiarly comforting. Unlike me, however, she had a profound self awareness and was certain of her footing in the world; a trait which I found particularly unnerving. But these parallel passions did not average out into an uninspired resignation of emotion. No, instead they served to enhance each other and keep my interest fiercely piqued in all directions, even in dreams, though it was in the uncanny hell of our similar pasts where we found each other most often and, even if briefly, we were in such rapture that we were able to forget that it had been hell at all.

Sophia always wore slightly oversized T-shirts and ripped black jeans with bright red Converse sneakers and she had shiny, straight black hair and her eyes were enormous and green and sad because they had been trained to look inward more than they were to look out. She was brilliant and innovative and when she allowed herself to laugh it was with great reservation, as though having once been wounded by her own forgetfulness. Every man who met her loved her, and she knew that, keeping only male friends around her and while I initially promised myself I would rather not speak to her at all than be relegated by her to the category of "friend", the magnetic pull she had on me offered me no choice. She was rather tomboyish and not sexy in any of the traditional senses, but as we grew closer and spent more time together I found her confidence and lack of restraint onstage wonderful and that wonder wove itself into a lustful desire for her and her hunger. I had discovered her in the same way a cartoon thief discovers an apple pie in an open windowsill—fatalistically drawn in by an undeniable and almost palpable arousal of the senses. After my set in Indianapolis that July as I walked back toward my bus, I heard her song booming out across what felt like the entire earth, and I immediately deviated off course to locate the source of a sound unlike anything. Suddenly there she was, her hair shining like new snow as it fell back and forth across her face with the smooth motions of a conductors hand, her eyes downcast but focused, her baggy Frank Black T-shirt wet with sweat and sticking in spots to her pale skin. Her voice was a plume of smoke from a smothered flame, both weightless and dim, and the lyrics she wrote were honest and specific, whereas mine—she said one night as we talked about Joyce while drinking boxed wine from a plastic cup weeks later—were masked in shadows

She touched my hand once while we stared at a lake in the woods behind an amphitheater in Pittsburg. As she talked about her sickness she put her finger on top of my hand, just gently enough that it could not be used against us in court, and I let it stay. Then she looked over at me and told me I should write a book. She said it would be "an affront to the universe" if I never in my life got around to doing so. I responded by asking her why she should not write one first.

"Because none of this," she said as she waved her other arm around her head "is my narrative."

"Yeah, well, I don't think it's mine, either. It belongs to the person who is watching me watch you."

"That's still you."

I said nothing in return, instead focusing solely on the tiny portion of her skin that met the tiniest portion of mine. All roads lead to that inch of flesh underneath her black fingernails and I stared intently at the point of our union, committing it so deeply and thoroughly to memory that it would never be forgotten. She told me she was sad that she appeared in my story when it was already too late. Then she withdrew her hand and flopped it carelessly back in her lap.

I had an inclination she was referring to my marriage, but I didn't ask what she meant because I knew that to give something a name made that something real and when something becomes real it has no other choice but to begin the slow process of death. For that reason I never told Sophia that I loved her, but as she stood above me one night in Lincoln, Nebraska offering her hand to help me up out of the grass where we had been laying on our backs watching the sky, I knew that I could. But there were also times that I wondered if she wasn't just a representation of an imprudent joy that I was no longer capable of experiencing in my heart and on the nights that I lay thinking about her that summer, I had trouble deciphering if she was the symbol or the meaning. The tablature or the sound.

But love for another person was no good anymore. It had no right being there in her company given the promises I had made before I was old enough to know that I might not know everything. So, the hours spent with Sophia would be vaulted away forever, kept from the world and preserved in a place outside of time where language could not deteriorate their appearance or replace their sheer might. We agreed never to speak again after that tour. So for a time, I remained static inside my own yard, too terrified to dance, only looking out at Sophia through a new fracture in the fence. I could see her twirling currents as they swelled at the mercy of the moon, trusting in something more pure than hard fact, free of any tradition or moral scorecards. And as her unbridled craving for life's secrets crashed against my vessel and a warm, clear mist made its way through that splinter, I was reminded that I had been locked out just as often as I had been locked in and I grew restless in my heart. Resentful. Hostile. In fact, I deserved a fucking medal for the restraint I had shown, not the cold shoulder from Hannah. My heroism in turning Sophia away warranted a parade and all I received upon returning home was scorn.

"What is your problem?" I shouted from beneath dented armor. Hannah was jarred into the moment.

"Don't talk to me like that," she said calmly. The serenity she maintained irritated me. It was flown in my face. It was an insult. I was incapable of such composure and she knew it. I scrambled for a cause to validate my rage.

"I haven't seen you in two months and you can't even be bothered to come and say hello to me?"

"Raymond, I was just enjoying the sun with Julius. Are you jealous of the sun? Am I giving it the attention you want for yourself?" Hannah laughed playfully. "Don't be such a child. Why don't you come outside and say hello to us?"

"Go to hell," I said as I stormed into our bedroom where I began unpacking my luggage, seething mad. Who the fuck did she think she was, talking to me like that? Did she know how many women would kill to be where she was, in Ray Goldman's apartment, sleeping in Ray Goldman's bed? How many other women would greet me with warmth and enthusiasm? Sophia would be proud of my music. Sophia would visit me on tour or come to see my shows. Sophia would fuck me. And Hannah didn't even look at me? Didn't embrace me? Didn't remember me? I lost Sophia forever and what did I get in exchange? A cold home with no one waiting for me inside of it. I sat down at the desk next to my bed and put my head in my hands and sobbed loudly, gasping often for air. I felt like I was the only man alive.

"You worthless fuck," I said angrily to myself. "You horrible fucking worthless cunt." I balled my hand into a fist and pounded it repeatedly into the side of my head with everything I had. "Horrible horrible horrible piece of shit. What the fuck is wrong with you, you stupid stupid fucking asshole fucking motherfucker." My head spun as my fist slammed into it over and over. I could hear the thuds echo in my bones and I could not hold myself back. Spit dripped from my lips. My body was in a rebellion against my brain that I did not have the muscle to quell. I was outside of my head and disgusted by what I looked down upon. Only when Hannah rushed in did everything converge and finally subside.

"No," she said.

"I'm sorry." I said into the crook of her neck, still weeping.

Hannah gently stroked my dirty hair. "For what?"

I saw Sophia. I felt her hand on mine. I saw her lips moving by the lake and her huge, sad green eyes. I could say it now, I could tell Hannah that I was man with new doubts and free myself entirely from the stifling weight of all those crimes. I could admit to her that I was a sinner and always would be. That I was weak and indecisive and scared and selfish and awful. But being honest would be far too difficult, so I did what I knew how to do best. I invoked the platitude of a coward.

"For everything."

"Shhhh." She kissed my forehead. "Don't be sorry, Raymond. It wasn't you."

Hannah had misunderstood.

CHAPTER THIRTY-ONE

THE BUS WOULD BE PULLING OUT OF Columbia, South Carolina earlier than usual after my show because a storm was moving into the Blue Ridge Mountains and our driver didn't want to be on the winding, dark roads in case the rain froze. I was told that over five thousand tickets had been sold that night and that we had done over thirteen thousand dollars in merchandise, but those numbers meant nothing to me anymore. They didn't excite me or fulfill me like they may have done for Frank. Instead, I felt ashamed. The less I wanted what I had, the more of it I seemed to receive, and that dichotomy had given me a severe distrust of the mechanics of god. It made me tread cautiously past my accomplishments while diving headlong into failure, fearing that any milestone might be provoked into rage if looked at too closely or for too long. Everything I earned felt like it had been stolen from the hands of those truly worthy and I slept lightly out of fear of being caught with hope in my possession. My contentment was just an open door through which only anguish would fit.

There had been a nervous tension in the venue that night. It crowded the room for the duration of my set and it caused me to struggle while trying to talk to the audience in-between songs. I fumbled over my words and time crawled. When I was finally done, the hired stage hands loaded us out and Cube belittled them as he oversaw the operation, verbally whipping them like horses to move faster. Even though bus call wasn't for another two hours, he was frustrated, as if we were running late for something that had been expecting us for centuries. When the room was emptied of people and beer bottles and the money was collected and the contracts were signed, he and Chet went directly to their bunks. They seemed concerned about something they either couldn't or didn't want to put into words.

With the bus driver still at his hotel, I was left alone in the front lounge in complete silence for the first time in years, and so I decided to try to meditate. I didn't know exactly how to do it but after reading the book Matt had leant me I was confident that I had a basic understanding of how to at least begin the practice—close your eyes and think of nothing. Easy enough. I sat up straight on the couch in the lounge on the passenger side of the bus and folded my hands in my lap, my left laying in the palm of my right, both thumbs touching. I closed my eyes and cleared my head.

I can attest to the fact that for a moment there was nothingness, though only in retrospect, for the instant that my awareness was directed at a particular stretch of time, the vacancy was eradicated by the presence of my awareness itself. Clearing my head of all static and signal—trying to cover the noise with a void—felt as futile as trying to stretch a small bed sheet across a large mattress only to have the corner opposite to the one you attended to become unbound, springing all other ends loose. Senseless images traipsed across the canvas and I could not settle. They were acrobatic and unruly, arriving without reason and disappearing without warning, baselessly unfolding into themselves with muted and ghoulish flashes of selfish fancy. They came uninvited. They left unconcerned. It was pointless to struggle against the ceaseless current of meretricious notions, I thought, for providing and processing images was all my brain knew how to do, how could I suddenly expect to know how to use it to ignore itself? It was irrational, and when things were irrational, it was my brain's job to make sense of it. I had no training, nor any reason to believe I could hush myself.

I will rest, I thought. *The book said rest is good. Just for a second.* I lay back on the couch.

I didn't intend to fully submit to sleep, but the quiet pulled me under and situated me at the base of the purr where I was given no choice but to worship. That majestic, awe-inspiring, but ever-dreaded hum. It rocked me gently at first. I was in heaven again. All was perfect, sung with a voice only I heard. Unfortunately, it was also temporary. My eyes rolled deeper into my head and the murmur slowly increased in volume and speed until my whole being was mixed into itself, all substances that had been poured into my skin were shaken rapidly like a cocktail. I panicked. My arms would not move. My eyes would not open. I would die. My lungs would refuse to take in air, my heart would not beat and all I was would cease to be. I must not succumb to death, I thought. If I were to die, then…

Then what?

I would be free. Hannah would be free. Loving Hannah as I did, my death was the greatest gift I could give to her, perhaps the only thing with any worth that I had left to offer. How could I have kept it to myself so selfishly for so long? Taking more willpower than it ever had taken to fight against the immovable mass of my worldly limbs, I gave up. I stopped building dams against the current of sound, and I let it all come rushing in, settling into the negative image of the void that swayed before me like a pendulum. I saw the driver board the bus and fire up the engine. I saw my heavy arms crossed over my rising chest. I turned around and looked upon my tattoos, my hair, my clothes, my face, my I. None of them were mine anymore. I felt nothing but hatred for it all. I turned again, and through the windshield of the bus I saw the rain that fell over the whole world for all time. I saw the driver as he gripped the wheel, as he locked his elbows, as his mouth opened to scream. And when he turned to look behind him, possibly hoping the sleeping body on the couch could do something—anything at all—I saw in his eyes a primeval fear. They did not represent horror, they were horror itself. Then I saw the guardrail split like a wishbone. I saw the room turn over. The ceiling at my feet. The ground above my head. The television ripped from the wall, shattering against the fridge. Windows imploded like stars as huge, dangerous branches of the trees that lined the hillside at once below us but now around us thrust themselves in to grab me, to warm me, to stroke my hair, to shake my hand, to get my autograph. I rushed past as I always did until the front of the bus collapsed like an empty can under foot and I was frozen in the light of a camera's flash. I saw it all but heard nothing. Then I saw no more.

A circular shelter poised along the bank of the freshwater creek running through the woods near my parents house appeared before me when my eyes finally opened. I had spent countless evenings foraging through those woods as a child yet I could not for the life of me recall having any awareness of the structure, though there it stood, as if it had been there forever. It was about twelve feet in circumference and its walls were made of thick branches cemented together with mud. There was a doorway, but no roof to protect it other than a canopy of leaves that the trees above provided. In my hands I held two pieces of fruit and a handkerchief. My mother, the healer, appeared at the entrance and waved for me to come inside.

"I can't leave," she said. "You have to come in."

"I forgot to bring the flowers,"

She smiled. "No you didn't." My mother took the apples out of my hand and led me across the threshold of the structure, above which was positioned the dead body of a small bird. Its wings were outstretched, its head turned to the side, its beak open, its lifeless tongue out. "My apartment. Now I remember."

Inside the hut was the living room of my apartment on Bollinger Road, except this version lacked all color. There was no paint on the walls, no stain on the wooden floor, no pictures hanging, and no furniture save for a table in the middle of the room upon which was an urn and a large ceramic bowl. All was grey and white, like the reverse image of a photograph I had taken. My mother placed the apples in the bowl and covered them with the thin cotton handkerchief. Then she lit a candle, kneeled down, and began to pray. I tried to listen but could make out no actual words. I kneeled down too and closed my eyes. All hushed.

When I opened my eyes, Claire was kneeling beside me in my mother's stead, but I was not scared by this transmutation. In fact, I somehow expected it, as if it were the next stage in a logical evolution of form.

"You will see Frank soon," she said. This news distressed me but Claire was reassuring, her voice without limits in its tranquility. It jostled awake a discarded archetype of love, one that springs forth when seen by the heart of another.

"Where is Lillian?"

"She was here long ago. Before any of us were even born. Do you understand that?"

I nodded. "And Evan? He lived in here, too."

"Evan couldn't wait for you any more, Raymond. You know that. He couldn't hold the door forever." She took my hand and we stood up. The old familiar table next to us reeked of varnish and was now littered with brass bells, hundreds of them, all varying in size and shape and heft and hue and smattered between them were small silver plates containing tiny piles of dust. Claire pulled a silk veil down over her face—it was red, the only thing of color—

and struck a match, then put the match to a pile of powder and rang a bell at random. The powder burst silently but vividly out of existence like mute gunpowder, leaving behind a stench of formaldehyde and as the air around the bell oscillated, Claire tilted her head to listen for a specific voice to reveal a long-awaited instruction. For a while none of them seemed to appease her or to bring her what she needed, but when she grabbed the handle of the largest golden bell and shook it, I felt the air that vibrated in its wake coil around my loins and I was immediately summoned to holy spasm.

Initially, I was humiliated and afraid, but the sensation was so powerful that there was no hope of disguising the act in secrecy as I had done for so many years. It stimulated entire planes of uncharted elation. The divine strength of the echo that trembled my bones was undiminished by time, growing even more fierce as it persisted. It was, after all, the sum of all human ecstasy and it knew not how to be denied. I attempted to internalize the personal rapture, to bite my tongue, to refuse to reveal my disgraceful addiction to forbidden joys, but it was too much. Without consent, I howled in utter euphoria.

Claire paused, nodded to herself, and put the bell down on the table.

As her body turned slowly toward me, the fear of being caught in the act of something so grotesquely human overwhelmed the orgasmic glory and my heart suspended its beating. I teetered on that intoxicating brink of darkness and light. Would she disown me? Would she expose me for the infant brute I was in my weakest moments? She lifted the red veil only slightly, just enough to see the bottom half of her face. It was the half kept from me the first time our eyes met.

Hannah.

Her mouth was open but as the deafening tone transmitted through her, her features stayed regal and composed. It was Hannah who made the sound that Claire had been listening for. Hannah herself was the instrument through which the music emerged. Hannah, my first and only truth, was the objective conductor of all harmonies. The wave guide.

She closed her mouth and the noise ceased. "Where you go, I will go." She said. Then she turned and walked away, a small white dog tagging along at her feet, bearing upon the horizon until their illumination became a pinpoint.

The den was dark now. I sensed I was no longer in my apartment, though I couldn't make out the details of anything particular as no light shone in from the sky above. There was a chair under me and it reclined the instant I named it as such. A distant but familiar voice passed through my head. Yes, I knew this place too. Dr. Singers office. Another hypnotherapy session.

Goddamit.

Resentment descended. I was back at the beginning of a long journey to nowhere. Hannah, Evan, Claire, even my own mother— all plants in a wicked joke to make me believe I had freed myself of the decaying rotation around the same horrible core. But I had not. I never would. After all, life was trivial and indifferent to men. I wanted to die. I was such a fool. There was no path away, there was just an enormous orbit that felt like a departure until it became an arrival again. Walking into that therapists office all those years ago was another foolish step along the same orbit that began when my life was shattered by Professor Tiller—that unexpected deviation which steered me off of my course and into a spiraling pattern of perpetual loss funneling us from prison city to prison city. I drag behind me into this world centuries of guilt and shame and the length of that tail only multiplies with every sick thought of escaping its burden. No therapy could extract me. How could a discarnate voice coming to me from outside of myself haul such misery off of my bones? It could not. Nothing from without could save me. Only something from within.

From within, rather than from without.

Could a small alteration in wording alter the world?

What if?

Here, at the fringe of my abyss, I had no other option but to start anew. I turned my back to the voracious two-headed animal of self-pity and doubt that snarled in those claustrophobic depths within me and began to silently hum Hannah's mantra as if clutching a life raft. I exiled all thought and memory and expectation, maintaining only the sound Hannah wrote for me, binding the tones to my inward breaths of damp air and passing it through myself in all directions. Stoic pillars of tranquility called down from their place in time by the focused vibration of one simple tone.

Unable to maintain grip for more than a few seconds, I was throttled back into my dream self at the bottom of the chasm by a soft pressure in the middle of my forehead, a tingling sensation as if a large bug had landed between my eyes. Attempting to swat it away, however, I found my hands were incapable of moving. My arms were pinned against the chair by several tons. My eyes too would not open. Sheer hysteria engulfed me as the mystic hum Hannah had planted in me swelled above a fault line to a volume that made it impossible for my body to hear the orders of my brain. It was another episode of sleep death, only this time I was not being kept from reentering the waking life of the world, I was excommunicated from my own dream, held captive in the limbo between two levels of my own subconscience. As I vigorously tried to shift the disconnected husk I was given in the trance, Hannah's once gorgeous harmony swept away from me like a cloud of atomic heat until its primal fury could carry it no further. When it finally toppled underneath its own magnitude, it buried the "I" beneath innumerable, simultaneous cries, and I could fight no more.

My awareness was too submerged to hope even for a return to a dream inspired by a life in the material world, let alone that profane world itself looming one story above it. Lungs refused to draw air and limbs vehemently denied the wishes of my tyrant mind. There was nothing left for me to do but accept my fate as it was and surrender myself to it. To trust its intelligence entirely. So I let it all go. I let go of all my wishes for something other than what I was given, for a deeper knowledge, for a better word, for a catchier song, for a truer love. The tension in my tired muscles began to disappear and I could feel pressure draining from me as if the ego were trickling out through a crack in the concrete.

Laying patiently in my new grave awaiting the inevitable opening of the exit—the very exit I had once thought to pry open with blade or poison or hasty leap down into the night—I again became acutely aware of a feint pressure against the skin between my eyes, as if someone was pressing their finger into my skull above the bridge of my nose. What began as a localized discomfort spread quickly across my face, radiating in concentric circles up to the crown of my head and down to my throat and my chest and my solar plexus and my spleen and my exhausted genitals and, with a pain unknown to any man a seedling appeared.

Though fragile, the new appendage tore mercilessly through my flesh, driven with the insatiable force of meaning, overcoming anything keeping it dormant, barreling into the ground above me like a diamond drill toward the center of the universe, past the worms and souvenirs of tragic ends. It grew upward from the fertile embryo of my dead self, producing and reproducing its own dimensions ad infinitum, effortlessly advancing toward the sun and the air where it knew it was destined to be before it ever was. It did not question itself, nor fear what was not itself. Then, dutifully and without pomp, the tip of the seedling breached the surface of the world in a morphogenetic field between soil and space, uttered its own arrival, and was known. Through that fledgling pinnacle I was given remote sight, a vision of what lay beyond the all. Pure love. Whole truth. Real beauty. Then a hunter.

You will see Frank soon.

Frank. The giver of names. The end-bringer.

He cackles. His shriek drowns out Hannah's voice.

There is no center. Black torrents of raw thought.

The hyena smells the air. Faith rots and Frank follows.

Hannah's voice. *Where there is lack, you will find him.*

So how do I keep him out?

Lack nothing. Love him.

No. Certain death.

Life is death. Forgive.

The flower awakens and opens.

Hannah is there. She is crying. I squeeze her hand and she is startled.

The doctors told me that two and a half months had passed since the crash, but I knew differently. Ages has gone by since I last visited this unnatural world of deceitful reflections, flashing in and out like burning embers of paper aloft hot air. I had seen more. What had been mine was mine no longer.

Both of my legs had been shattered, a lung punctured and my right arm broken. My head had been shaved in order to stitch together the part of my scalp that was ripped open by broken glass. It would take months of physical therapy to stand again, but it was only when I was told that Chet and Cube did not survive that I cried, though, because I am human and I am terrible, and so I cried not for them. I cried for myself who was unfairly detained in this maze of anguish by the miserable deeds of flesh. I cried out of frustration over the inabilities of my calloused hands to create goodness. I cried for the ineptitude of my voice to praise the divinity I required knowledge of in order to be just. I cried for the incapacity of my heart to ever know heaven. My human eyes had been teased with momentary glimpses of the glorious infinite that lay beyond this sphere. Chet and Cube had moved into the absolute without me. And so I cried. I had seen the garden in which they now flourished, the paradise that life on this earth had kept me out of. I offered myself to the grave, and it passed me by. There is nothing more wretched than a man refused by death.

CHAPTER THIRTY-TWO

I **PUT TOURING ON HOLD FOR ABOUT NINE** months in 2011 in order to work on a third record. Chet and Cube would go back to their jobs as local sound engineer and bouncer for a few weeks while Frank would get back on the road as a guitar tech for The Killers thanks to a mutual friend at their management company who thought to call Frank when a job position unexpectedly opened up. When Frank informed me of this opportunity, he assured me that it was in my best interest, that the bands younger fan base was a new and naive demographic that his internet notoriety could entice into the venues I played when he eventually came back to work for me, as if he were some cyber pied piper leading the innocent children to a salvation they didn't know they wanted. Of course it went to serve his ego as much as it did my career, but it was harmless and when presented as such, again, what could I say that didn't sound completely unappreciative? Eddie, however, saw something wicked.

"I told you that pudsucker was not to be trusted." He said as we drank at Father Baker's on a cold April evening.

"What?"

"He fucking used you."

"No, he did not. He's my friend. We're partners."

"Bullshit. He's an opportunist. He owes everything he has to your music and he doesn't even acknowledge that."

"Eddie," I said. "I don't care what Frank does in our off time. If he wants to make some money while I take time off the road, it's his life. He works hard. More power to him."

Eddie turned his barstool toward me and I could see now a thin patina of intoxication draped over his eyes. He dug his pointer finger into my chest.

"The need Frank has for validation and for some sense of perverse immortality is very fucking real and it is very fucking dangerous. He will cut you down if given the chance. How do you not see this yet? How does nobody fucking see this?" He slammed his hand on the bar with each syllable out of sheer frustration with having a vision he could not describe to me. "I've been warning you not to trust him since day one." I winced and rubbed the spot on my chest where his finger had dug in.

"This is just your new '9/11 was an inside job' thing. You say shit all the time that isn't true to get a reaction out of people. I know you never liked Frank but I promise you. He's not using me."

"Okay, man. Enjoy your time off while he's on a tour that you weren't even asked to play. And jet fuel burns hot enough to melt steel. Give me a cigarette."

Frank came home at the beginning of October with just enough time to prepare for a short tour of Australia before the year ended. When we left that fall morning to arrive two days later in the spring, Hannah cried in our doorway and I promised to call as soon as I could, as I always did. I then got into a rented van, picked up Frank, Cube, and Chet from their apartments and drove the four of us to New York City where we caught a plane to Los Angeles where we drank Bloody Marys on our brief layover until we got on a plane that touched down in Sydney. Sixteen hours, seven jack and cokes, three action movies, and four percosets later, our heads foggy and our bodies tired and sore and covered in a film as if the sickly breaths of all the other passengers had settled on us like dew. We had not only lost an entire day of the calendar year, but the airline had lost two out of three guitars, the one given to me by my father included. As Frank and Cube and Chet berated and argued with everyone from desk clerks to shift managers to security guards, I lamented on a bench outside of the Duty Free shop in the Sydney Airport arrivals zone.

At least for the time being, the guitar I had been given by my dad was gone. The one that gave me all the elements I had needed to mold a spinning globe, the kin that listened when I spoke, the elder that sang when I needed consolation, the scribe that had recorded every whim, was missing, and there was nothing I could do about it except accept. I felt as if I had lost something more alive and with more function than a mere tool; I had lost both a map of my past and a key to my future. We had given each other purpose and I could no longer protect it as I should have done. Something that intrinsic to who I was should not have been left alone to suffer such disgrace. I should have been there to hold it. I should have bought it its own ticket and sat next to it on the plane as we looked forward to our first tour of a brand new continent. I should have been there to guide it in.

After a dozen overseas calls to my management, we eventually left the airport with a wire transfer from my label for one thousand dollars to buy enough equipment to finish the five-show tour that was scheduled for Sydney, Newcastle, Melbourne, Adelaide, and Perth. According to the Australian promoter Nigel, who would serve as Cube's assistant and occasionally our tour guide, these were the only cities worth hitting on your first run, but as you become more popular you can eventually make your way further inland and even to some spots up North where the rooms are harder for newer acts to fill due to the scarce population of anyone even remotely interested in American music.

The van that Nigel drove from the airport to the hotel sped deftly along the coastline as if applying brushstrokes to a canvas which would eventually merge into a whole portrait of a new world. I had seen beaches and trees and the Pacific Ocean before, but not these particular beaches and not these particular trees and this particular ocean was never on my left as we journeyed south. The further we traveled, the more I felt I was consuming a fruit that couldn't possibly taste as sweet ever again. I savored every stretch of highway we traveled over, biting off entire mouthfuls of succulent fruit after a famine of a hundred years. Our enthusiasm for such newness was unabashed. Chet smoked out of the window in the passenger's seat which was on the wrong side of the car that moved on the wrong side of the road and sang abrasively to whatever song came on the radio while Cube laughed on the phone with a friend back home. When he hung up and all was silent again, Frank looked up from the game on his cell phone to ask the typically ignorant tourist question with an earnestness that belied his patronization of things unfamiliar to him.

"Is that where AC/DC grew up?" he asked to an underwhelmed van as we passed a very typical home on our way toward the hotel. "Is this where Silverchair ate?" he asked as we passed a McDonalds to a crowd now becoming disgruntled at the lack of originality. "Did Crocodile Dundee buy a knife there?" as we passed a sporting goods store, this time to a group of people who couldn't care less about his faux brazen stupidity. Sensing that he had already annoyed everyone around him, he grew louder and fired off even more absurdities about Men At Work, Vegemite, Mel Gibson, fighting kangaroos, and koalas with herpes. We all shifted uncomfortably, but Nigel faked a laugh with every disingenuous inquiry as any good guide should, and because of the polite but awkward encouragement that what Frank was doing was actually good, Frank continued on until every puff of air was out of Nigel's sails. It wasn't until he quoted "Dumb and Dumber" that Cube finally snapped and told him to pipe the fuck down. Frank smiled proudly at what he considered to be a small victory over nothing specific.

"How's the blow here?" Chet asked Nigel after a few seconds of quiet.

"Mate, you mean cocaine? There's almost none of it. This is an island. You can't make it. And who is stupid enough to bring it in their luggage?"

"You're saying that the cocaine market is untapped?" Chet asked excitedly, his eyes wide.

"Will," Nigel went on, "you can find some. I can find you some if that's what you're asking. But it's going to cost you a small fortune."

"So, if you sell coke here you have a few small fortunes." Chet stated as a fact.

"Will, basically yes." At this, Chet erupted.

"Ray, I love you, but fuck you. I quit. I don't punch a clock in heaven. I'm gonna be rich."

The Grand Sydney Hotel was about two hundred meters from the famed Opera House, which looked to me like a pile of old conquistador helmets haphazardly discarded at the end of a pier by a bay. Seeing something so familiar to you through magazines and television shows take on a new dimension of space is an odd experience, one that left me wondering if I should genuflect at its base or take a thousand pictures to prove to others that such a marvel did exist in our world before the marvel disappears. The hotel was positioned on a boardwalk bedecked with bars and restaurants, one of which Chet walked to the second the van was valeted.

"I'll be in there. Come and get me if you need me," he said, and took off before anyone could object. Holding Chet's luggage, Nigel checked us in at the desk, and after a brief conversation with the clerk about the closest place to buy a few guitars, he turned and handed us each keys to our own rooms, mine being a harbor side suite on eighth floor, while the rest of the guys were given rooms on the floors below me—Frank somewhere on six, Chet and Cube both on seven. This was inconceivable to me, as even on support tours of arenas in the states, I had no other option but to share a large room with at least one other of my guys, if not all three of them.

"We have our own rooms?"

"You have your own apartments," Nigel said. "Don't fuck it up like some fuckin' bogan. Cube and Frank and I have to go buy you your new equipment. Meet in the lobby at five p.m. I'll take you to sound check."

I took the elevator up to the eighth floor and when the door to 807 opened it revealed a room bigger than the condo I lived in back home. It was something I always dreamed of, something I always knew I deserved. The kitchen that was laid out immediately to my right as I walked in was typical of a loft apartment, but the fridge was stocked with champagne and wine instead of baking soda and weed cookies or old food Hannah cooked that we never finished eating. Straight down the hall was a living room with a couch that could be folded out into a bed in case there were more people than there was sleeping space (which there undoubtedly would be that night) and a glass coffee table which was perfect for Chet's priceless piles of cocaine. To the right of the living room was the bedroom, through the bedroom to the right was a bathroom with a whirlpool tub and out the bedroom to the right was a sliding door next to the living room couch which lead out to a balcony. I set my bag down, unlocked the door and stepped outside as amazed as I would have been if I had just set foot on another planet.

I walked to the railing. I closed my eyes and let the wind move my hair in any direction it chose, anchoring me in a moment that I had entirely to myself, which no one else had, feeling invincible and vindicated. When I opened them, the view of the Harbor Bridge across the cove from me made any picture I could have taken of it seem like a man's feeble impression of a warrior giant. Below me people bustled. Ferries blew their horns. I leaned over and looked eight floors straight down at the group of beautiful men and women dressed in linen huddled around a table drinking martinis on a chilly but bright autumn afternoon, seeming to very much enjoy their version of the world that was so much the opposite of mine. And yet, there we all were at the exact same time because like me, they too must have been entitled to such bountiful spoils.

The fall from here would definitely kill you I thought, before finally turning and going inside.

CHAPTER THIRTY-THREE

AFTER TWO WEEKS OF OBSERVATION IN the hospital I was allowed to return home, though this news did nothing for me. My new homesickness was not a hunger for the comfortable familiarity of my living room, but had instead transitioned into an urge to venture somewhere off the grid. Life itself had been demystified and in the wake of the bus accident, I recognized it as nothing more than an uninspired farce looping endlessly on the clock of a preoccupied caretaker like an old movie played in the rec room of a mental ward. All of it was for naught. All of it.

Hannah attempted to care for me, running only on the fumes of her vestigial graces and I could sense with clarity that her days of nobly performing thankless acts of unconditional love were nearing their end. She had come to symbolize the savage cruelty of an indifferent universe, one that mindlessly devoured hope like a starved reptile consumed flesh, its behavior driven by a terrible instinct that was too swift and effective to be reasoned with by anything whose death was so imperative to its survival. She had not asked for nor deserved the dreadfulness that I had fettered to our commitment, though it was on her table alone that the brutal fates had unfairly heaped it, and it became obvious to me that she could not bear my burden much longer. She had already raised one animal. I had been emotionally unavailable for years and now that the last fragment of a normal marriage had been stripped from her by an inanimate piece of twisted metal that snapped my bones, she hovered lethargically. We no longer abided the same flow of time. Hers was frantic and shifted sporadically between her past and present like the arm of a polygraph test, while mine moved as slow and as aimless as litter trapped in the eddy of a stream. The only thing that held us together was the exclusive kind of sickness we shared. From the other room I could often hear her weep. She was more broken than I.

Save being hosed down in the parking lot like a muddy vehicle, I could not properly clean myself in my own home as there were only showers, nor could I reach into the cupboards, fridge, or microwave from a seated position in order to feed myself. Hannah had been demeaned for too long to be assigned the awful task of attending to my useless body, so the decision was made to move me back into my parents' house which had been modified to accommodate my wheelchair-bound sister. While I would recover and receive physical therapy in my parents home, Hannah would continue living in our apartment with our dog where she would sleep soundly for the first time in her life, for once assured that I was not entangled in the distant arms of another woman when I wasn't next to her in our bed.

Using an electronic chair that carried my body up and down my parents staircase I moved back into my old room at the end of the hallway on the second floor in the summer of 2014. It was smaller and more drab than I remember it being, though all of the enormous, vivid memories, like sneaking girls through my window or discovering the music carved into new records, had been hauled out to make room for the self-loathing teenager that moved in after being kicked out of Virginia Tech and his seriousness still lingered in the air. My parents home was a museum that preserved the historical objects of angst, and my parents were its diligent caretakers, both of them suspended in a common disbelief that it could one day be returned to its original glory if they just kept working.

Undoubtedly sensing the inhuman gloom that took up residence under his own roof once more, my father had taken it upon himself to move a large refurbished table into my room and situate it against the wall underneath the window that looked out over their backyard. On top of it he had placed my laptop along with some notebook paper, pens, and a few books from his collection that he thought I might enjoy.

"What's this?" I asked as I wheeled into the room after a particularly grueling therapy session.

"It's a writing desk."

"For what?"

"For writing."

"But writing what."

"I don't know. Lyrics? It will be good to keep your mind active while your body recovers." I laughed mockingly. My father winced.

"I'm not writing lyrics. That part of my life. It's over. I can't sing. I'm done with it."

"Yeah. Well." He paused. "That might not be your decision." He stepped around behind me and pushed my wheelchair up to the desk, my weak and faulty legs fitting surprisingly underneath.

"See? It's a match. Like cogs in a gear."

I felt bad for laughing in his face and searched for something gentle to offer up. "I'm sorry I ever lost your guitar, dad."

"I never had one. That guitar was always yours. I'm sorry it lost *you*." Then he left.

I immediately recognized the writing desk as my father's repurposed workbench from the basement. Though the computer was placed where the instruments would lay with their insides hanging out like patients undergoing invasive surgery and the pens and paper and books were in the spot where his old screwdrivers and soldering iron used to be, this was unmistakably the same one. When I was young I would stand at his side in the dank cellar under a solitary bulb hanging from the ceiling, just barely tall enough to see up onto the elevated plane where the transformation occurred, and watch him as he added pickups to old acoustic guitars in order to make them electric. I didn't necessarily understand what he was doing, but I didn't dare interrupt his process with foolish questions. I was content to simply observe, reveling in the magic of witnessing one thing becoming something entirely different in my father's deft but heavy hands.

CHAPTER THIRTY-FOUR

THE VENUE IN SYDNEY WAS CALLED "THE Field," and as we pulled up to it in time for sound check, we found a line outside the front door stretching around the corner hours before the doors even opened to ticket holders. Hundreds of people on the other side of the world anticipated my performance that night. The pride that swelled within my heart was unmatched by anything in recent memory. No love was as rewarding as that of a crowd's, no sound on earth more singular than that of hundreds of men and women cheering.

"Oh, I get it," Chet said as Nigel pulled the van around back to the loading doors. "Ray, you're 'playing The Field.' Like you're prowling for sex. Very lurid. Very clever."

After we loaded in and began sound check, I immediately discovered that the strings of the new guitars had not been properly tuned. I asked for Frank's assistance and I was told by Chet from the front of house that he had been in the lobby drinking with some of his fans since we arrived. I of course was infuriated at his this notion.

"Can someone get him?" I asked over the microphone "Cube? Will you find Frank and politely ask him to do his fucking job?" As Cube marched off the stage toward the front hallway I removed the guitar and handed it to Nigel who was standing at the side of the stage behind the monitor board. Then I went upstairs to my dressing room and drank a beer while I paced angrily like a caged lion. After that I drank another one. Then another. Fifteen minutes later someone knocked.

"What!" I yelled. The door opened and Cube stepped inside.

"They're tuned. Come finish checking."

"Fuck no. I'm not on Frank's time, this is MY show. Sound check is over and if it remains undone then it is entirely Frank's fault. He doesn't get paid tonight. You got me? You take three hundred dollars off his fucking take home for not doing what I hired him to do"

"Okay," Cube said. "Now pump your brakes. It's my job to worry about Frank. Not yours. Don't let it ruin our first show here."

"MY first show here." I snapped. "People around here seem to be forgetting that. Nobody would be here if it wasn't for me. Certainly not Frank and his fucking circle jerk of a fan club." Cube backed out of the room and closed the door. I drank alone for hours. At 9:00 p.m. I took the stage.

There were no considerable problems for the first few songs of the set. The crowd was responsive and I felt confident in my voice and in the voice of my guitar, but it was as I tuned up to begin the fifth song that a D string broke and everything else broke with it.

"Shit," I said into the mic. "Give me a second, guys." The clock began ticking down. I took the guitar off and instinctively turned to my right where I had expected to see Frank waiting in the wings with a backup guitar tuned and ready to go, but Frank was not there. Nobody was. I looked around, dumbfounded. *You're losing them*, I thought. Nigel who was working the monitor board shrugged. I was alone on an island.

"The fuck is Frank?" I mouthed to him. He kept his shrug going.

After a silence which felt like hours, I saw Chet approaching me from side stage. He put his hand on my shoulder and whispered into my ear.

"Just keep smiling. No matter what. Frank said that since he is not getting paid tonight he was not going to work. He's at the front bar with some friends." At this my mind went blank. I was hijacked by a breed of anger which I had not seen in years. It fell over me like a veil, absconded with my body and replaced it with a carnivorous savage, free of kindness or reason. I threw my guitar down, smashing it into pieces and charged off the stage, parting the befuddled crowd as I rushed to the back of the room like a wildfire through dead brush. My purpose was in the lobby bar and I would not be stopped before finding it.

The order of events that transpired next I cannot recall specifically. I may have swung first, though I vaguely remember Frank turning his attention away from a conversation, seeing me descending upon him and preparing himself, fists raised. What I will never forget, however, is the repose that I saw in his eyes as I grabbed his collar and drew back my only weapon. It was the kind of cool that only those who have accepted a conclusion are capable of possessing and it ended all wars before the first shot had been fired. I flinched in its awful presence. I doubted for one measly second. One second. But that was all he needed.

Blurry, ringing, dreamlike. A soft impression of an otherwise crisp earth.

The sounds made by onlookers were muffled and unorganized, packed carelessly into the air, lacking any true context, content or order.

The sky above me. Damask clouds. Red wine funneled upward to fill their blank spaces.

No. That's a carpet. Not wine. Blood.

A vulgar snap. Dead wood. Ribs.

I gasped for air and fell over onto my back.

I just need a minute to remember the parameters. What it was supposed to look like, what I had always known it to feel like.

This is not right. I am still partially in the dream. In the underworld. I have not fully surfaced.

Frank sits above me now and I am relieved. He too is from there. I am not alone anymore. Thank god. He is screaming angrily, but I cannot hear. My nose cracks like the shell of an egg and I taste rust.

I know you Frank. Do you recognize me? We are brothers and what you know I know too. Help me up.

No words.

Franks hands disappear.

What an upside down game this is where Frank the artist has no hands.

Poor Frank. We are opposites here.

Air moves further away, and though the screaming of my ribs rattles my blood, I try to draw breath back from over the stretch it has covered.

Franks mouth begins to move but I only recognize the shape of a few sounds.

Save your breath Frank, please.

I cannot hear you anyway. There are no tones.

We will never get out if you use up all the air.

Deeper. Deeper.

I will see you soon, Frank. And when I do, it will be for all time.

Until, again, nothingness.

When I woke up I was laying on the couch in my dressing room. Cube and Chet were above me and someone I only kind of recognized was waving a pungent stick like a sorcerers wand in front of my face.

"Hey, Rocky," Chet said, smirking. "Does this mean no encore?" Instantaneously the memories came flooding back. Frank had beat the living shit out of me in front of a crowd of people.

"Where is he?"

"I had Nigel drive him to the airport," Cube said. "He's on the next flight home, and as long as I'm around, he's not coming back." I tried to sit up but a pounding in my head prevented it.

"Okay."

"Do you want to go to the hospital?"

"No. I want to finish the show."

"Ray. Show's over."

"Fuck. Take me back to the hotel."

"Sure little buddy," Cube said. He sent the promoter who was still holding the smelling salts to bring a car around. The man nodded and vanished, then reappeared a few minutes later, letting us know it was waiting for us outside.

The ride back to the hotel was silent, because the rage I had felt on the event horizon of the fight with Frank was replaced by a perfect vacuum once I awoke on the other side. No sadness. No passion. No concern. No memory of shame nor residual hostility. There was simply nothing, a nothing so thorough and absolute that I wondered if maybe I wasn't actually on the other side just yet. Maybe I was still plummeting through something unknown toward something unknowable.

When I got back to my hotel room, walking through the lobby and in and out of the elevator with the help of Cube and Chet, they laid me down on the couch. Chet opened the balcony door to let the warm, fresh air in. Then he stood there next to Cube awaiting instruction like an obedient dog.

"Give me a little bit. I'll be fine. We'll figure out what to do about the rest of the tour later. Go get a drink downstairs. I'll call there if I need anything."

"Well, okay," Chet said. "If you *insist* I go get drunk, I will. But remember, it's only because I want what's best for you." Then they left.

I lay there trying to come to terms with the nullity that lingered. The things he said to me, the words he so carefully chose to pierce my flesh as he beat me were too much for me to bear, too heavy on my head to ever crawl out from under, whether he was in my presence or not. He thought so ill of me for so long. He hated me and always had hated me. I was still as sorry as the day we met. All the while his dense fists raining down upon me in a timeless repetition as I lay on my side and tried to shield my head and face, as if those were the valuables that needed the most protection.

He was too right to ignore. I was nothing, had nothing. Everything was broken. His resentment was ever reaching, his hatred for me more pure than virgin blood. Tears welled in my eyes. Everything I thought I knew was wrong. As mindlessly as I had charged off stage to meet my inevitable end, I stood up from the couch and walked out onto the balcony through the escape hatch that Chet had opened for me. I climbed over the railing and, gripping it with both hands behind my back, I leaned out over the edge, peering down at long last through the mouth of the black hole I had been falling through since the day I was born.

Even if I had been angry enough, I understood that seeking revenge on Frank would never be sufficient. At best, even if I could convince him that he had been wrong in the opinions he had formed of me throughout all our years together, it would only blur the details of the crime perpetrated by my existence in the mind of one meager witness to it, it would not be the undoing of the crimes caused by existing itself. But by letting go of the metal rail that stood as the only obstacle between this world and no other, I could, in one fell swoop, eliminate all spectators. All of my fans. Anyone that had ever known me or thought they knew me would vanish. Not a single person would survive my fall and no bystander was as good as no crime.

As I stood there looking down at the throngs of people so impervious to the fatality that they were all about to experience in a reality so fundamentally similar to theirs that it might as well be comprehensive, I became aware of a sadness—the first palpable, nameable thing I had felt all night. But it was not a sadness for the mother earth I once so adored that would be unfairly forced to simultaneously mourn all of her children that never even made it to my thirty-first birthday, it was a sadness for the innocent soul that was unfortunate enough to choose me and which was now unable to make provisions for its trek back across the bridge between "was" and "is not". If one was to receive word that they were sick and that their days among the living were numbered like Eddie's father had, then the process of death would begin with the brain's recognition of all those implications, and as the body grows weaker and the prospect of the future grows more dim, the mind and soul most likely work harmoniously with all of nature to ensure that when the heart eschews beating, death is simply the final step of process that the entirety of the world has been adequately prepared for. What was true for Eddie was true for my mother and father and I, who had secretly and pitifully accepted Lilly's death when told of her incurable condition. It was the kind of acceptance that may have allowed us brief moments of joy with her in our flashes of forgetfulness but nevertheless hungover our household ever since her fledgling soul mingled too early with nonbeing in some baffling process, long before that soul may have been fully ready to transition from an old world to a new. By falling into the street below me, the only preparations I could make would be closing my eyes and tensing my muscles mere seconds before passing through the concrete, through the center of infinity and back into nonbeing. Neither I nor my family could pray nor confess nor confide. So without the full consent and readiness of my mind and my flesh and my bone and my blood, would my soul enter its old home as crippled as Lilly's had entered her?

I leaned back, turned carefully around and hoisted myself over the railing and onto the balcony once more. *Fuck Frank*, I thought. He may have caused me to lose my footing but I could not let him force me to lose myself. I went back inside, called down to the bar and told Cube that the rest of the tour was cancelled, that I needed to go home to recover indefinitely. To this day I have no idea if it was doubt or faith that brought me in off that ledge.

CHAPTER THIRTY-FIVE

HANNAH LEFT ME IN NOVEMBER, JUST AS the last leaves of the tree outside my bedroom window fell, burrowing crudely through the biting air to rest atop an earth that was by now too cold to break for proper burial. Seeing her sickly limbs exposed as they were I found it hard to believe that I was ever unknown enough to confidently crawl into them without fear of being dropped.

There were undoubtedly thousands of contributing factors as to why Hannah went her own way, but an accidental pocket dial a few years earlier which allowed her access into a conversation between Sophia and I about a book we had both read convinced her that she no longer reigned absolutely over the riotous kingdom of my hard heart. She said she heard in my voice that night a passion that she found unfamiliar and that she could sense a fire burning in a place from which I returned to her carrying only a cold wind.

"You never talked to me about books, Raymond." She said as she stood against the wall of my bedroom, I, sitting in my wheelchair near my desk. "You never talked to me about anything. You didn't let me in and I can't just keep knocking forever. You gave so much to so many other people that there was nothing left in you for me." She covered her mouth and looked out the window into herself while I peered down at my useless feet. The truth of my neglectful inconsideration of my wife was more horrible than any infidelity I could have committed or any lie I could have told to over it up. A crude current swept in from which nothing idyllic could be salvaged.

"Did you love her?"

My eyesight became blurry. "I don't know." I said, though I knew. I had never loved anything as well as I had loved Hannah in that brief moment of the bright flash before the bulb went out. Not even Hannah. I shook my head and looked up at the ceiling. I owed her something, some reason for what I had done but I found only words.

"I think I learned to just." I struggled "To love myself through her."

At this Hannah burst into tears. "If you wanted to know how to love yourself, why didn't you just ask me to teach you. I was the first one who ever knew how to love you, Raymond." Hannah was sobbing now, covering her face in her trembling hands. "I would have taught you. You never asked me." When I reached up to touch her she pulled back.

"I wasn't worth all this. Why did you stay?"

She picked nervously at her fingernail and looked again out the window where she met her meaning in midair. "Because I deserved to be punished for loving someone as blindly as I did." She wiped a tear away from her face as it fell, a more radical act of valor than any I had ever remembered seeing from her. Hannah had understood after all. She and anyone foolish enough to offer me their love ought to incur the wrath of a vile god, ought to be stricken from a world which had proven itself unfit to be fair. To confess fondness for me was to align oneself with heedlessness and that made one damnable, if not already damned.

"I have to go, Raymond. I have to go." I could sense that there was an aura of madness coming on. "I have to go, Raymond. I don't belong here anymore. Me and Julius are going to my parents. Do not call me."

It took not force to reanimate the delicate frame that Hannah had been trapped inside of for so many years, but an unceremonious acceptance of the annihilation she had been made to watch and a genial faith in the fertility of her own ashes as only Hannah could know. In separating herself from me she was able to face forward and move gorgeously into being, transforming into the type of person that I could have stayed with forever. Hannah bent over, kissed the scar on my head, and was gone. In the same room where we had been fused by young passion we were now cleaved by ripened grief. The spiral downward through pasts and futures and figures and proofs and light and dark and calamity and calm and echoes and songs had finally approached a singularity. Looking back over the top of the seat that day in the auditorium, Hannah had become a pillar of salt and I the splenetic flame that hungrily ravaged the entire world she built with nothing but miracles of hope. Loss upon loss upon loss until only I remained.

After all had gone, I saw no sun and heard no voices. I served the dismal waking hours of my exile yearning only for something sacred and in the few cruel minutes of sleep that mocked a famished captive of this plane, I dreamt of nothing but her. For days I refused food but the pitiful sight of my beaten parents had somehow divined a place of compassion in my arid being and so, after a week of fast, I was finally convinced to eat something, which I did regretfully, knowing that to consume meant only to grow and to grow meant only to struggle and to struggle meant only to age and to age meant only to die and every time I died I became so tired of the repetition of the nihilistic sermon of chaos and increasingly more disgusted by the unfairness imbued in such a predictable composition that I never would have fathomed taking that first step again had it not been for the sadness in their eyes.

The walls and the carpet of my room were of the same listless hue as the perpetually bleak sky during the winter that stretched into the early part of March, the edges between the parameters built by hand, fusing seamlessly with those set in place by predestination. There were times when I sat at my desk staring blankly outside that I could not be certain if the world was the room itself or if the room itself was the whole world. It just seemed as if everything blanketed by the sky was an extension of the things I had immediately available to me, like the tips of longer fingers, all senses of heaven riled by the nerves of a common earth. Everything was equipoised.

One night in May as the leaves loyally returned to the trees in order to shield me from the presumptuous gaze of surrogate wraiths, I hurriedly returned to my room from dinner in order to attend to a melody that had appeared from nothingness. My legs were growing so strong that I needed only one crutch now, and my hair was returning near the scar that spanned the entire right side of my head like foliage around the place of a great fire. The pictures of Hannah too, though still stunning, were less intense then they had once been, as if mixed with softer shades by the days that passed and the anguish I had outlived. I had lost the sound by the time I put pen to paper but as I sat at my desk fighting to rediscover the channel that carried the tone, I took notice of a book Sophia had lent me during the summer in which we met by no coincidence that was stacked on a pile along with many others, Matt's included. I opened it for the first time ever and found that she had written something on the inside of the front cover.

"there is a reason he did not call this book 'Hermine.'" —S

I thought about her fondly for a moment and the way she looked that night in Lincoln as she towered above me against the backdrop of innumerable stars, her hair the same darkness as that of infinite depth and woven equally as determined into the tapestry of my wicked lives by the tender hands of slow time. Then, instinctively, I closed the book and hung it up with the others. I was still very much unprepared for the conclusion that her narrative might bring, the conclusion that the beginnings of all narratives bring. But if I ever did find new purpose and write a story like Sophia had implored, I knew I would first have to decide upon a name.